Their bodies

CW00391679

As she lost her
caught and stea
strong arm.

'S-sorry,' Bridie stammered breathlessly.

'No need to be—ninety per cent of all accidents occur in the home,' he observed, smiling down at her.

Jack was still holding her, and as she gazed up into his deep brown eyes her heart quickened at what she saw there.

'Beautiful Bridie,' he murmured, brushing back a stray tendril of hair from her forehead with a feather-light touch. 'Beautiful Bridie McEwen, why do you try so hard to hide it?'

Maggie Kingsley lives with her family in a remote cottage in the north of Scotland, surrounded by sheep and deer. She is from a family with a strong medical tradition, and has enjoyed a varied career including lecturing and working for a major charity, but writing has always been her first love. When not writing she combines working for an employment agency with her other interest, interior design.

A QUESTION OF TRUST

BY

MAGGIE KINGSLEY

DID YOU PURCHASE THIS BOOK WITHOUT A COVER?
If you did, you should be aware it is **stolen property** as it was reported *unsold and destroyed* by a retailer. Neither the Author nor the publisher has received any payment for this book.

All the characters in this book have no existence outside the imagination of the author, and have no relation whatsoever to anyone bearing the same name or names. They are not even distantly inspired by any individual known or unknown to the author, and all the incidents are pure invention.

All rights reserved including the right of reproduction in whole or in part in any form. This edition is published by arrangement with Harlequin Enterprises II B.V. The text of this publication or any part thereof may not be reproduced or transmitted in any form or by any means, electronic or mechanical, including photocopying, recording, storage in an information retrieval system, or otherwise, without the written permission of the publisher.

This book is sold subject to the condition that it shall not, by way of trade or otherwise, be lent, resold, hired out or otherwise circulated without the prior consent of the publisher in any form of binding or cover other than that in which it is published and without a similar condition including this condition being imposed on the subsequent purchaser.

MILLS & BOON, the Rose Device and LOVE ON CALL are trademarks of the publisher.
Harlequin Mills & Boon Limited,
Eton House, 18-24 Paradise Road, Richmond, Surrey TW9 1SR

© Maggie Kingsley 1996

ISBN 0 263 79497 0

Set in Times 10 on 11 pt. by
Rowland Phototypesetting Limited
Bury St Edmunds, Suffolk

03-9603-48543

Made and printed in Great Britain
Cover illustration by Alexis Liosatos

CHAPTER ONE

BRIDIE gazed at her senior partner in clear dismay.

'But Simon looks forward to helping me out at the practice when you go on holiday, Andrew,' she protested. 'He loves it—you know he does. He says it's the only opportunity he ever gets to talk to patients—normally they're fast asleep on his operating table!'

Andrew Weston thrust his hand through his shock of white hair ruefully. 'I know that, my dear, but Jack's the son of one of my oldest friends, and when I heard he was at a bit of a loose end at the moment I thought—'

'You thought I could wet-nurse him for a while,' she sighed. 'Oh, Andrew, I need an experienced doctor to help me while you're away—a doctor who knows the area—not some spotty-faced kid fresh out of med school who'll spend half his time phoning the surgery to say he's got lost.'

'Jack's not—'

'What did Simon say when you told him we wouldn't be using him this year?' she demanded.

'He was fine—said he quite understood.'

'Well, lucky old Simon.'

Andrew chuckled. 'Look, it's only for three weeks, Bridie, and Jack's an excellent doctor. In fact, he's—'

'Spare me the eulogy,' she interrupted as she followed him down the stairs. 'I'd rather find out what kind of doctor he is for myself. So when's this boy wonder due to arrive?'

'Some time this afternoon. I thought he could have the green bedroom—'

She caught his arm quickly. 'You've asked him to stay *here*?'

Andrew stared at his shoes uncomfortably. 'It seemed a bit stupid to put him up in a hotel when there's so much room in this big old house of mine.'

Bridie groaned. 'So not only am I going to have to put up with this Jack. . .Jack. . .?'

'Jack Culrain.'

'Jack Culrain all day, I'm going to be stuck with him in the evenings as well? No wonder you waited until the last possible moment to tell me!'

His lips twitched. 'Let's just say I guessed you wouldn't exactly be over the moon at the idea.'

She shook her head. 'You're a coward, do you know that, Andrew Weston? A nine-carat lily-livered coward!'

He hung his head, and despite her annoyance she began to laugh. 'It's no good you standing there pretending to be all apologetic when I know damn well you're not, Andrew. I hope your maggots, or whatever those disgusting things are that you use for bait, fail to attract even so much as a tadpole this year; I hope you break your favourite rod—you deserve some punishment for landing me in it like this.'

'It will be all right, Bridie, I just know it will,' her senior partner declared as he began piling his suitcases into the boot of his car. 'Jack's very likeable, and you won't have to entertain him or anything—he's used to shifting for himself.'

'He'd better be.'

He paused uncertainly, recognising the tone in her voice. 'You be pleasant to him—do you hear me, Bridie? The last thing I want is him throwing in the towel after a couple of days.'

She opened her eyes wide. 'Why, Dr Weston, anyone would think you're suggesting I'm some kind of ogre.'

He grinned. 'You're soft as butter with your patients, my girl, but I've seen you in a temper if you think someone's not pulling their weight and it made even my poor old heart quail, I can tell you.'

'Is Dr Culrain a sensitive soul, then?' she murmured, her eyes gleaming. 'Oh, the poor diddums.'

'*Bridie*!'

She chuckled. 'OK, OK, I promise I'll do my very best not to upset his delicate young ego. Just remember this, Andrew,' she added as she closed the car door after him, 'you owe me for this—and you owe me big!'

Andrew's deep, throaty laugh drifted back to her as he drove away.

It was all very well for him, she thought vexedly as she went back inside the house and up the stairs. He was going to be safely out of the way, sitting by some peaceful loch, while she was left to carry the can with a newly qualified doctor who was a stranger into the bargain. A locum like that was going to be no help at all in a rural Scottish practice where nobody bothered with such mundane things as signposts or house plaques.

A malicious smile crossed her face. The first time this Jack Culrain got lost she'd leave him to stew in his own juice for a couple of hours, and that would teach him to arrive uninvited and unwanted.

Her smile disappeared, however, as she collected some fresh sheets from the laundry cupboard and took them through to the green bedroom. It made sense to have this Jack Culrain stay here; it made sense, but it didn't mean she had to like it.

In the five years since she'd joined Andrew in his Perth-shire practice she had come to regard his home as her own, and now her comfortable, quiet existence was

was going to be disrupted by the arrival of some over-eager young doctor brim-full of the latest ideas.

She frowned deeply, and then shook her head and chuckled out loud. God, she was beginning to sound like some middle-aged, disapproving matron, and she was only twenty-nine—correction, she'd be thirty in a couple of months, but she was getting to the age when those few months mattered.

'Come on, Bridie,' she told herself firmly as she made up the bed and began tidying the room. 'It's no big deal. In three weeks he'll be gone and things can return to normal.'

Within half an hour she was finished and stood back to survey the room with a critical eye. It looked neat and tidy, and that was about all a locum could expect.

'Not exactly welcoming, though, is it?' she murmured.

Her irritation struggled with her better nature and her better nature won. Quickly she went down to the garden and picked a few flowers. She doubted whether Dr Culrain would even notice the touch but at least it salved her conscience to have made some effort for him.

She had scarcely put the flowers by the bed when she heard the sound of a car coming to a halt outside the house—the sound of a very rough car indeed. Curiously she pulled back the curtains, and saw what had to be the oldest, rustiest Ford ever to have passed its MOT sitting in the driveway.

Her lips curved into a smile. She'd had a car exactly like that when she'd first qualified. It had spent more time in the local garage than it ever had on the road, but how proud she had been of her first set of wheels.

All at once her antagonism deserted her. She could just picture what this locum would be like—so young, so nervous, so anxious to please—and swiftly she ran down the stairs and threw open the door, a welcoming smile on her face.

'Bridie McEwen? I'm Jack Culrain—the locum.'

Her first thought as her eyes took in the hip-hugging denims, the checked shirt that was stretched over a muscular torso, and the face that wasn't young or spotty or nervous was that she was going to kill Andrew. This was no boy just out of med school, but a man of at least thirty-five—and Andrew should have warned her, prepared her.

Her second thought was that no amount of warning could have prepared her for meeting Jack Culrain. He was without doubt the handsomest man she had ever seen. He had thick black hair, a deep tan, and a pair of liquid brown eyes that were regarding her with some amusement.

'Do you think I might come in?' he said. 'Or is the threshold as far as a lowly locum ever gets?'

She muttered something incoherent in reply and stepped aside, a faint flush of colour on her cheeks. She was definitely going to kill Andrew when he came back from his holiday. Why hadn't he told her? Why hadn't he corrected her false impression? At least she might have stood some chance of appearing her normally cool, professional self instead of standing gaping at Dr Culrain like some adolescent schoolgirl.

'Big house,' Jack commented as he followed her along the hallway towards the stairs.

She pulled herself together quickly. 'Andrew bought it shortly after he got married. He and his wife were hoping to have a family, but when they discovered they couldn't he converted the ground floor into a surgery, dispensary and office. The living-room, kitchen, study and bedrooms are on the floor above.'

'And just the two of you live here?'

Was that criticism or just curiosity she heard in his voice? She couldn't be sure.

'Just the two of us live here, yes,' she replied. 'Would you like to see the surgery and dispensary, Dr Culrain, or would you prefer to unpack first?'

'Unpack, I think—and please, call me Jack.'

She nodded and led the way up the stairs.

'I understand Andrew's been a widower for almost ten years.'

'His wife died of a heart attack nine years ago.'

'And you've been here five?'

There it was again—that tone she couldn't quite identify. 'You ask a lot of questions,' she declared.

He smiled. 'Just nosy, I guess.'

'Then the first thing you'd better learn is that in this house we respect one another's privacy,' she replied curtly.

It was one of the things that had so warmed her to Andrew Weston when she'd first joined him. He'd asked no questions and she'd appreciated his reticence. It had been a comfortable, healing five years—becoming part of the community, becoming accepted—and the last thing she wanted was someone asking questions, prodding at old wounds.

Aware that Jack was gazing at her curiously, she quickened her pace. 'The sitting room's in here,' she continued, opening the door. 'The kitchen's next door and your bedroom's just across—'

'Bridie—that's not a Scottish name, is it?'

'My mother was Irish.'

'It's pretty—like its owner.'

'I'm glad you approve,' she said evenly.

'Oh, I do; I most certainly do.'

She turned round quickly, but the sharp retort that had been on her lips died in her throat. He was smiling at her with such warmth that all thoughts of saying anything at all deserted her. Deliberately she took a firm grip on herself.

'Here's your room. The furniture's a bit on the old-fashioned side. . .' She came to a halt, angry with herself. What on earth was she doing apologising for the furniture? She and Andrew liked its shabby, solid comfort.

'It's fine. There's just one thing,' he added as she turned to go. 'I don't suppose there's any chance of my exchanging that single bed for a double one, is there? It's my height, you see,' he continued apologetically. 'If I lie crosswise in a double I just about fit. In a single my feet stick out over the end.'

Bridie wasn't surprised. She had always thought of herself as tall, but standing next to Jack Culrain's massive frame even she felt dwarfed.

'You could have this bedroom if you want,' she said uncertainly, crossing the hallway. 'It's smaller, and it hardly ever gets any sun, but it does have a double bed.'

'You're sure it would be no trouble?' He smiled.

To her acute annoyance her heart gave a treacherous leap. That smile was devastating.

'It's no trouble at all,' she said firmly, opening the laundry-room door and pulling out some double sheets. 'I'm afraid the room's a bit on the dusty side. I'll give it a clean later—'

'There's no need; I'll do it.'

She could not disguise her surprise.

'I'm a New Age man, Bridie—I cook; I clean—'

'Sew?'

'Hey, have a heart,' he protested, his eyes dancing. 'I said I was a New Age man, not a paragon!'

She chuckled. 'Well, Mr New Age Man, you can help me make up this bed.'

He nodded and followed her into the bedroom. 'Andrew tells me you were a real high-flier at university—top of the class in everything it was possible to be top in,' he observed.

'Did he?'

'Said he reckoned you could have any job you wanted.'

'Andrew's a great flatterer,' she replied coolly.

'So what's a nice girl like you doing in a place like this?'

Her eyebrows rose. 'I can't believe you actually said that!' she exclaimed. 'That chat-up line's so old it's got whiskers.'

'Sorry,' he said meekly, though he looked anything but. 'But what *are* you doing here?'

'Making up a bed?'

He grinned. 'Sharp as well as pretty—a good combination. Come on, why not tell me a little bit about yourself? I like to get to know the people I'm going to work with.'

There it was again, the insatiable curiosity—the curiosity she meant to nip firmly in the bud.

'If you're wanting any lunch I think we'd better just get on. There's no duvets, I'm afraid—only blankets. How many would you like?'

'Three, please.'

She opened the blanket box at the foot of the bed.

'So where's Andrew off to on holiday—somewhere warm and exotic?'

He was doing it again—still asking questions. But at least, she thought with relief, they were now on safer ground.

'He's fishing at Laggan.'

'But that's only—'

'Thirty miles away,' she nodded with a smile. 'Don't ask me to explain it, but he's booked into the Royal

Hotel every year for his holidays for as long as anyone can remember.'

'Wouldn't it be cheaper for him just to stay at home and drive there every day?'

She laughed. 'Of course. But I think half the fun is staying with old friends, reminiscing about the fish that got away, and if it makes him happy who are we to criticise?'

'And what about you?'

'Me?' she said in confusion.

'What makes you happy? Presumably this area, as you've been here five years.'

'I like it here, yes,' she said, her voice tight. 'Soup and sandwiches suit you for lunch?'

'Sounds great—I'm starving.'

'Cheese and tomato, or ham and pickle?'

'Ham and pickle. You've family connections here, then? Is that why you're here?'

She straightened up from tucking in one of the blankets, half-angry, half-amused at his persistence.

'You're just not going to give up, are you?' she declared. 'All right, then; if it's my biography you want, here it is. My name and Irish connection you know already. As to my age—that, Jack, is none of your business!'

A wide smile lit up his face. 'Go on.'

'My father was a Scot—from Edinburgh not Perth-shire—and he died when I was a baby. My mother worked all the hours God sent, cleaning office buildings, so that I could stay on at school and then go to university to study medicine.'

'And you're very proud of her,' Jack said gently.

A faint shadow appeared in her eyes. 'One of the biggest regrets of my life is that she didn't see me graduate. She died during my third year at university, you see. When I qualified I worked in a practice in

Kelso for two years, and then I came here. There you have it—one potted biography.'

'That isn't potted, it's positively truncated!' he protested. 'Where are all the essentials, like the men in your life—'

He came to a halt as she bent to pick up the quilt. For a second he'd seen real pain in her eyes, and he cursed himself inwardly. Somehow he'd touched a raw nerve, and he found himself wishing that he hadn't.

'Look, Bridie, if I've said something—'

'Your turn now,' she said brightly—too brightly. 'One biography, please.'

'OK,' he declared, relieved that the awkward moment seemed to be past. 'Born in Suffolk thirty-six years ago—unlike you I'm not coy about my age. Parents both English and both doctors, so mealtime conversations weren't exactly riveting. Father still alive, mother not. Educated at boarding-school—'

'Very fancy.'

'Oh, there was never anything but the best for Jack Culrain,' he replied lightly, but his eyes, she noticed, were bitter. 'After university I worked for a while in a practice in Winchester, and then it was off to Canada, South America, Europe. I'm just back from a two-year spell in Italy.'

That, she thought, explained his incredible tan.

'Several girlfriends—nothing serious,' he continued. 'And there is not, nor is there ever likely to be a Mrs Jack Culrain. There you have it—one biography as requested, and a considerably fuller one, I may say, than yours.'

'So you're between jobs at the moment?' she said, deliberately ignoring his jibe.

'I'm off to the States in three months.'

'You certainly get around,' she observed. 'Which is it—itchy feet, or are you working on the principle that a moving target's hard to hit?'

'Who's being nosy now?' he said, his eyes dancing.

As an answering smile was drawn from her she sighed inwardly. Why did he have to be so damned attractive? Why couldn't he have looked like the locum she'd imagined so disparagingly, or even have been like Andrew—sturdy and jovial and unthreatening? She could have handled that. But this man—this man was something different altogether.

'I'll leave you to unpack,' she said quickly. 'Come across to the kitchen for some lunch when you're ready.' And with that she was gone, leaving him gazing thoughtfully after her.

For a second Jack stood motionless, and then shrugged his shoulders, went over to the bedroom window and gazed out—a narrow grey street, a few clustered houses, and then fields, more fields, and some high hills beyond.

He grimaced slightly. How Andrew Weston could possibly have endured practising medicine here for over thirty years he couldn't imagine. The longest he'd stayed anywhere had been two years, and always he'd been anxious to move on. No commitments, no long-term relationships—that had been his life and he liked it that way.

He sighed as he began to unpack. He'd worked in worse places in his time but he hadn't actually planned on working in Britain at all this summer. He had thought to stay with his father until he went to the States, but two weeks of each other's company had been more than enough to convince both of them that they preferred one another at a distance.

When Andrew Weston had suggested that he fill in for him while he was away he'd jumped at the offer, but what he hadn't banked on was the area being quite so sleepy and isolated.

His unpacking completed, he went out into the hallway, only to stop as a flash of bright colour caught his eye. Sitting by the single bed in the room opposite was a forlorn vase of flowers. It didn't take much intelligence to guess who had put it there and he picked it up and carried it through to his room, a slight smile crossing his lean face.

She was a strange one, this Bridie McEwen. All starchy efficiency on the outside and yet underneath—underneath he was sure that it was an entirely different story. His smiled widened. Perhaps it wasn't going to be quite so sleepy here after all.

'Anything I can do to help?' he asked as he entered the kitchen and found her busily making sandwiches.

She looked up and shook her head, and the flippant comment he had been about to make about a woman's place being in the home died on his lips. Sunlight was streaming through the kitchen window, illuminating her face, and he realised with a sudden shock of surprise that she wasn't simply pretty, she was beautiful, and yet for some strange reason she was doing her damnedest to try and hide it—trying and failing.

Her shapeless grey suit might be unflattering in the extreme but it could not disguise her incredibly long and slender legs. Her skin, scrubbed clean of all make-up, might be too pale but its paleness merely accentuated her huge eyes—eyes that were neither blue nor grey but a sort of heather-colour in between.

Even the severe chignon she had pulled her hair back into didn't work. Stray tendrils of glossy chestnut hair defiantly escaped the confines of the chignon to curl round her slim neck and onto her wide fine cheekbones—curls he found his fingers itching to reach out and touch.

Abstractedly he shook his head. How could he not have been aware of it before, that nothing short of a paper bag could hide that stunning face?

Aware of his scrutiny, Bridie frowned. 'Something wrong?'

'Not from where I'm standing,' he said, with a lazy smile. 'From where I'm standing there's absolutely nothing wrong at all.'

To his surprise a deep flush of colour appeared on her cheeks as she turned away to switch on the kettle with a snap. Surely she must be used to receiving compliments? And yet he was virtually certain that not only was she embarrassed by his remark she was also angered by it.

'Tea or coffee?' she said brusquely.

'Coffee, please—I'm hell to live with unless I get a massive injection of caffeine every day.'

Bridie said nothing, but her mind was working overtime. Somehow she had to get this situation onto a more professional footing. She was the partner in the practice, he the lowly locum, and it was about time he understood that.

'By the way,' he continued, easing himself up onto the worktop beside her, 'I forgot to ask you earlier—is there a garage I could put my car in?'

'There's one round the back, but do you think your car would make it that far?' she said, far more tartly than she'd intended.

His face lit up with genuine amusement. 'It's a dreadful old rust-bucket, isn't it? It seemed a good idea to buy something cheap for the three months I'm going to be in Britain, rather than hire a car for that time, but I have to say I'm having grave reservations about my decision. The damn thing broke down four times on the way here.'

She found herself relenting. 'The local garage hires

out good, reliable cars at reasonable rates—and you're going to need a reliable car round here. Tell them I sent you and you should get a discount.'

'They owe you a favour?'

'Bill McLeod, the owner, does. I cured his haemorrhoids.'

Jack started to laugh, and she did too.

'Tomato soup or lentil?' she asked. 'It's just tinned, I'm afraid.'

'Lentil's fine—here, let me get it for you,' he added, reaching past her as she stretched up to take a tin from the cupboard.

Their bodies collided momentarily, and as she lost her balance she found herself caught and steadied within the circle of a strong arm.

'S-sorry,' she stammered breathlessly.

'No need to be—ninety per cent of all accidents occur in the home,' he observed, smiling down at her.

He was still holding her, and as she gazed up into his deep brown eyes her heart quickened at what she saw there.

'Beautiful Bridie,' he murmured, brushing back a stray tendril of hair from her forehead with a featherlight touch. 'Beautiful Bridie McEwen, why do you try so hard to hide it?'

Her whole body quivered and seemed to melt against his as he drew her closer. Slowly he lowered his lips towards hers and then it came—the overwhelming panic sweeping up from nowhere, the blind fear she'd been so sure that she'd mastered, and she jerked out of his arms quickly.

'As soon as I've got a spare minute I'm going to have to work out some kind of rota for the kitchen,' she declared, amazed at how natural and calm her voice sounded when she felt anything but.

'A rota?' he echoed, puzzled.

'We can't both use this kitchen at the same time—we'll end up permanently under one another's feet if we do.'

'I see what you mean,' he said, irony clear in his voice as he surveyed the kitchen, which could more than easily have accommodated a family of six. 'So what do you suggest—I use it from seven-thirty to eight o'clock in the morning and then from seven to eight at night?'

'Something like that,' she mumbled, all too conscious of how stupid her suggestion sounded, but knowing too that the less time she spent in this man's company, the happier she'd feel.

'And if I transgress—stay five minutes longer than I should—what happens then?' he asked meekly. 'Do you stand me in a corner, or put me over your knee and spank me?'

She flushed hotly. 'Certainly not—'

'Pity,' he replied, his brown eyes gleaming. 'I think I could get to like that. What about the bathroom arrangements?'

'We have two, so we won't have to share.'

'No?' He both looked and sounded crestfallen.

Bridie bit her lip. He was laughing at her, she knew he was.

'While you're here I think it would be best if you stuck mainly to surgery duties,' she declared quickly, desperately trying to restore the situation to a more professional footing. 'Not knowing the area, it can be very easy to get lost—'

'And you wouldn't want me to?'

Her frayed temper snapped. 'Quite frankly I could cheerfully see you at the far side of the moon at the moment, Jack Culrain!'

'And there was I, thinking you liked me,' he sighed.

'Will. . .will you stop it?' she cried in frustration. 'You seem to think this is all some huge joke; well, it isn't—not for me. The only reason you're here is because Andrew, for some benighted reason known only to himself, felt sorry for you. You are not—nor would you ever be—my choice for this job, and I tell you this—if you don't pull your weight, if you're as lax with the patients as you seem to be in. . .in everything else, I'll bounce you out of here so fast that your feet won't touch the ground—got it?'

He gazed at her silently for a moment and then his lips curved into a smile. 'Tell me something, Bridie. Do you ever wear your hair down?'

She opened her mouth, shut it again, and then turned on her heel and banged out of the kitchen.

Why couldn't she effectively silence this infuriating man? She'd never had any trouble in the past in inflicting a crushing snub, a biting retort, when anyone tried to get past her defences. Why was she so apparently incapable of doing it now? Because, Bridie McEwen, you're attracted to him, she thought ruefully; because you don't really want to shut him up completely.

She dug her nails deep into her palms as images from her past rose up to haunt her and a small voice whispered mockingly in her ear, It's no use, Bridie; no matter how you feel, it's no use.

The clatter of the front door jerked her mind back to the present. 'Fiona, is that you?' she called over the banister.

'Who else were you expecting—Mel Gibson?'

Bridie chuckled with relief. Fiona Ross had been Andrew's receptionist for the last sixteen years, and, despite being small and plump with short blonde curls and a pair of laughing eyes, Bridie had seen her single-handedly oust even the most high-powered of salesmen. She would be more than a match for the persistent Jack Culrain.

'Simon arrived?' Fiona asked as she came up the stairs.

'There's been a change of plan this year,' Bridie said ruefully, but before she could elaborate the kitchen door opened and Jack came out, a wide smile of welcome on his face.

'You'll be Fiona Ross?' he said, holding out his hand towards her. 'Andrew's told me all about you.'

'I deny everything,' Fiona declared, her brown eyes shining.

'Pity.' He grinned. 'I was hoping at least half of it was true!'

'Who *is* this?' Fiona laughed, glancing across at Bridie.

'Jack Culrain, the locum,' she replied coolly.

'You know, there's got to be something in the water round here,' Jack continued, his eyes on Fiona with obvious approval.

'Something in the water?' the blonde repeated.

'How else can you explain why every woman in the place seems to be beautiful?' he commented.

Bridie threw her eyes heavenwards in disbelief at such a corny observation, but to her dismay Fiona giggled like a teenager. So much for her hopes that Fiona would put him in his place, she thought with irritation.

'I'm going to grab a quick shower if that's all right, Bridie,' he continued. 'I'll freshen up a bit before you show me the surgery.'

'You'd better make it quick, then,' she replied. 'Afternoon surgery starts in half an hour.'

He nodded and disappeared across the hall.

'Wow!' Fiona exclaimed, her eyes large with admiration. 'Is that some hunk of a man or what?'

Bridie chuckled despite herself. 'He's certainly nothing like Simon, is he?' she said.

'I'll say not. For one thing Simon could never fit into a pair of jeans like that.'

'Simon would give himself a hernia if he tried to get into trousers that tight!' Bridie laughed. 'Oh, Fiona, what on earth am I going to do with him?'

Fiona's eyebrows rose suggestively and Bridie shook her head. 'I want *sensible* suggestions, Fiona! He's impossible. He treats everything I say like a huge joke; he wouldn't know the word "discipline" if it came up and hit him in the face. How can I work with someone like that?'

'You know perfectly well that Andrew wouldn't hire anyone who was useless, so why not just enjoy him being here? I'm certainly going to!'

'May I remind you that you're a happily married woman with two children?' Bridie pointed out primly.

'Yes, but that doesn't mean I'm dead from the neck down.'

Bridie laughed again and then sighed wryly. 'So much for me hoping you'd be on my side.'

Fiona groaned. 'You haven't had a row with him already, have you? He's gorgeous, Bridie. Don't scare him off, as you have every other halfway decent-looking bloke who's come into your life.'

Bridie said nothing, and Fiona gazed at her with sudden concern, all laughter gone from her face.

'Oh, Bridie, not every man you meet is going to be like Cameron,' she said gently. 'Just because—'

'Could you get that for me?' Bridie interrupted as the phone in the kitchen began to ring. 'I'd better open the surgery.'

'Bridie—'

'The phone, Fiona,' she called over her shoulder as she went down the stairs.

Three weeks, she thought as she unlocked the surgery door; I've only got to put up with him for three weeks. God, it sounded like a lifetime—a lifetime with a man who was too unsettling, a man who was continually asking questions she didn't want to answer, making her face facts about herself that she didn't want to face.

'Who was that on the phone?' she asked as Fiona appeared at the surgery door.

'The police.'

A cold chill crept round Bridie's heart at the look on Fiona's face. 'What is it, what's wrong?'

'It's Andrew. He's been in a car crash, and it sounds bad, Bridie—really bad!'

CHAPTER TWO

'Both of his legs are broken, he's fractured some ribs, and he's sustained whiplash injuries to his neck. But all in all, when you consider his age and the fact that his car's a total write-off, I'd say Andrew's been damn lucky, Bridie.'

'You're absolutely certain he's suffered no internal injuries—there's no sign of pulmonary collapse, no brain damage—?'

Simon Morrison got to his feet quickly and came round his desk towards her. 'Bridie, he's going to be all right. We brought him down from the theatre about an hour ago and he's sleeping peacefully. I'm not saying he's going to be up and about in a couple of days, but I promise he'll make a complete recovery in time.'

She buried her face in her hands, the worry and strain of the last few hours finally catching up with her. 'I thought I'd lost him. I thought. . . I was so afraid—'

Her voice cracked and Simon patted her shoulder awkwardly. 'Andrew's not ready for a pair of wings and a harp yet, Bridie—apart from anything else, he'd drive the other angels mad.'

A hiccup of unsteady laughter came from her. 'You're a good friend, Simon,' she declared, blowing her nose vigorously. 'A good friend.'

'And you're worn out. Go home and get some rest. There's nothing you can do here.'

'Can I see him first?'

'He's still pretty groggy from the anaesthetic—'

'Please, Simon—just for a minute.'

He shook his head wryly. 'You're just not going to be convinced he's OK until you see him for yourself, are you? All right, then—but just for a minute, no more.'

Quickly Bridie followed Simon out of his consulting room and along the corridor towards the wards, relief flooding through her.

She had driven like a maniac to Perth Hospital, convinced that she would find Andrew if not dead then not far from it, and all she had been able to think about was how empty her life was going to be without him. Slowly but surely, without her even realising it, she had come to rely on her jovial senior partner, to value both his company and his advice, and the thought of losing him had appalled her.

'He looks pretty hellish, Bridie,' Simon warned as he stopped outside a private room. 'His body's taken quite a battering and there's masses of tubes and wires all over him—'

'I'm a doctor, Simon. I know what to expect.'

'Clinically you do, but emotionally it's an entirely different story,' he said gently. 'This isn't just a patient, this is Andrew, and it makes a big difference. In you go—but don't stay too long. The pair of you need to rest.'

She nodded and disappeared through the door.

'Simon Morrison?'

Simon turned to see a tall, muscular man striding down the corridor towards him. 'Yes, I'm Simon Morrison,' he replied, his eyebrows raised questioningly. 'And you are. . .?'

'Jack Culrain.'

'Ah, the usurper.'

'Sorry?'

'So you should be.' Simon smiled. 'I'll have you know I look forward to my yearly foray into the world of general practice, and you pinched my job!'

There was no animosity in Simon's voice or his grey eyes, and Jack grinned. 'How is Andrew?'

'Quite remarkable when you consider what he's been through.'

'Injuries?'

Briefly Simon outlined them.

'And Bridie—how's Bridie?'

'Shattered. She's with Andrew now on the strict instruction that she's not to stay long. Perhaps you can persuade her to go home and get to bed—I haven't had much luck yet.'

'I'll try, but I can't promise anything,' Jack said wryly.

Simon chuckled. 'She's independent-minded is our Bridie. Had a flea in your ear from her yet?'

'Should I have done?'

'If you don't give one hundred per cent to the practice you will. The girl's a workaholic, and she expects the same kind of dedication from everyone.'

'But you like her?'

A nurse came towards them, pushing a trolley laden with medicines, its wheels squeaking and rattling in the still corridor.

'On the night-shift again, Liz?' Simon declared.

She blushed furiously. 'It pays well, Simon, and the patients don't argue back—what more could a nurse ask for?'

He laughed. 'Nice girl, Liz Howard,' he observed as she disappeared into Men's Surgical. 'Widowed three years ago—left with two kids to bring up on her own.' Aware that Jack was waiting, he sighed slightly. 'Look, I more than like Bridie, but she made it clear she wasn't having any so I've settled for just being her friend.'

Jack gazed at him thoughtfully. Late thirties, brown

hair, grey eyes, tall, and with a ruddy, open complexion. Simon Morrison wasn't handsome, but he had a pleasant face and, as a surgeon, excellent career prospects. Most women would have jumped at the chance.

'And you're happy with that—the friendship-only bit, I mean?' he said.

Simon spread his hands expressively. 'I didn't have a choice. If you don't accept what Bridie is prepared to offer she freezes you out entirely. I'm a patient man, though; I can wait.'

'I wish you luck.' Jack smiled. He knew he should leave it there; he had no right to pry, to ask questions, but he just had to ask. 'Tell me something, Simon; what do you know about Bridie—her background, her past?'

'I know she has the most amazing curriculum vitae I've ever seen, and that's about all anyone knows about Bridie. She's a very private person.'

'So I've discovered.'

'Getting interested yourself?' Simon asked, his grey eyes fixed on him.

'Hell, no!' Jack exclaimed. 'I'm just passing through.'

Simon nodded, but Jack had the uneasy feeling that he was being scrutinised.

So Simon considered him a possible rival for Bridie, did he? If the situation hadn't been quite so ridiculous Jack would have laughed. He'd always made it a policy never to get involved with a woman who didn't know the rules—a woman who wasn't happy to accept that any relationship they formed involved no commitment on either side— and no one who blushed as adorably and with such clear confusion as Bridie McEwen could possibly fall into that category.

There had been a couple of times in his past when

he'd made mistakes—mistakes that had led to angry scenes, uncomfortable recriminations—and he had no intention of repeating the experience on the strength of a pair of heather-blue eyes and a wealth of chestnut hair.

'Happy now, Bridie?' Simon asked as she emerged from Andrew's room.

'Happy,' she murmured, but it was clear that she was more shaken than she cared to admit.

'Jack's come to make sure you get off home,' Simon continued.

'Jack?' she repeated, a slight frown appearing on her forehead.

'You really know how to boost a fellow's ego, don't you?' Jack grinned, noting the pallor of her skin, the dark shadows underneath her eyes. 'I'm your locum—we met this afternoon, remember?'

She smiled slightly. 'I remember now—the spotty-faced kid. Private joke,' she added, seeing his look of bewilderment. 'How long do you think it will be before Andrew's fit to return to work, Simon?' she continued, turning to him anxiously.

'Three, possibly four months.'

'Four *months*!' Bridie echoed, the enormity of her situation suddenly hitting her.

'I can stay on until I go to the States, if that's any help,' Jack declared. 'I've nothing else planned.'

'I couldn't possibly ask you to do that,' she said swiftly, knowing that what she really wanted to say was, If you were the last available doctor in the entire country, Jack Culrain, I wouldn't ask you to do that.

'Look, even if you advertise for someone immediately you'll have to wait a while before the replies come back, and then there'll be interviews to conduct,' Jack said firmly. 'Surely it makes sense for me to stay on for as long as I can?'

Bridie's heart sank. Of course it made sense, but how was she going to cope with his presence for three whole months when she hadn't thought that she could endure having him around for three weeks?

'What do you want to do, Bridie?' Simon asked quietly, sending a searching glance towards Jack. 'With Andrew out of action, you're in charge—it's your decision.'

'What Jack says makes sense. . .'

'But?' Simon prompted.

She looked from him to Jack. What choice did she really have? She couldn't cover the practice on her own, and if Andrew had considered Jack good enough to replace him while he was away on holiday then he was obviously the first choice to fill the gap for longer.

If she said she didn't want him he would undoubtedly want to know why, and that was something she couldn't tell him. All right, so he was handsome and charming, but the world was full of men like that—was she going to run away from them all? She made up her mind.

'If Jack's willing to stay on until I can find another locum then I'd be very grateful,' she said.

And an advertisement for his replacement is going into the medical journals first thing tomorrow morning, she thought firmly.

'Right, now that's sorted out I want you to go home—'

'I could really murder a good, strong cup of coffee first, Simon,' she interrupted.

He gazed at her with clear exasperation. 'The only place you'll get a coffee at this time of night is from the machine in the hospital canteen, and the best that can be said for that is that it's wet and warm. OK,' he continued, with a sigh, seeing her crestfallen expression, 'Jack will get you a cup of coffee—and then, for God's sake, get her to go home, Jack,' he added under his breath. 'What she really needs is sleep.'

Jack nodded.

'Thanks for all you did, Simon,' Bridie said quickly as he turned to go.

'Hey, it was all in a day's work.' He smiled.

'Thanks, anyway,' she murmured, reaching up to kiss his cheek. 'I won't forget.'

Jack took her firmly by the elbow. 'The canteen awaits,' he said, steering her deliberately away from Simon. 'One wet and warm coffee coming up.'

'I'll see you soon, Simon,' she called over her shoulder.

'Any time,' he replied, a slight frown appearing on his forehead as he watched them go.

'God, how I hate hospitals,' Bridie declared, her nose wrinkling with distaste as she led the way to the canteen.

'Isn't that a rather strange admission from a doctor?' Jack exclaimed.

'Why do you think I'm in general practice?' she replied. 'I can't abide the white coats, the white-tiled corridors, the antiseptic smell. I always think it's like being in a reformatory for recalcitrant inmates rather than a place of healing.'

'You really *don't* like hospitals, do you?' he laughed, opening the canteen door and standing aside to let her go in ahead of him. 'How do you take your coffee?'

'Black—no sugar.'

As he went to get it Bridie sat down at one of the tables. The canteen was deserted except for a group of junior doctors, and a general air of squalor and despondency hung over the place.

Empty paper cups and plates littered the tables, and remnants of curled up sandwiches and pork pies mingled with discarded apple cores and orange peel, but Bridie saw none of it. All she could see in her mind was Andrew wired to an assortment of monitors; Andrew so white and frail; Andrew looking suddenly so old.

She shut her eyes quickly, desperately trying to shut out the image, to blot out the sounds the machines he had been attached to had made.

'Are you OK?'

She glanced up quickly to see Jack standing in front of her, his face concerned.

'He swerved to hit a rabbit, Jack—a *rabbit*! He could have been killed—'

'But he wasn't.'

'He crashed headlong into a wall,' she continued, as though he hadn't spoken. 'His car is just one tangle of unrecognisable metal. The police say it was a miracle he survived. When I think of what could have happened. . .'

He quickly put down the coffee he had in his hand and caught her firmly by the shoulders, forcing her to look at him.

'Bridie, listen to me. Andrew's had a horrific accident but he's not dead. Yes, I know he's going to be out of action for some time,' he continued as she made to speak, 'but he's going to recover; he's going to get well—hold onto that thought.'

A small sob broke from her. 'I know—I know that. It's just. . .it's just. . .'

Tears began to trickle slowly down her cheeks and instinctively he knelt down and took her gently in his arms. She shifted slightly in her seat and for a moment he thought that she was going to pull away from him, but she didn't pull away. She leant her head against his shoulder and curled her hands onto his chest like a small child seeking refuge.

But she wasn't a child—the softness of her body and

the sweetness of her perfume told him that. He reached out a hand to stroke her hair and suddenly she sat bolt-upright, consternation plain on her tear-stained face.

'Oh, my God, Jack—my patients!' Her eyes searched for the canteen clock and a groan came from her. 'It's ten o'clock—*ten o'clock*—I've missed both afternoon and evening surgery—'

'I took them for you.'

'*You* did?' she exclaimed.

'I am a qualified doctor, remember?' He grinned.

'I know,' she said, with a wry smile, 'but I can't apologise enough. I didn't even tell you I was leaving—I just went. Talk about behaving unprofessionally—'

'You were worried,' he said softly.

'That's really no excuse. I shouldn't have abandoned you like that, with no warning or advice. I just seemed to forget about everything—all I could think of was Andrew, of getting to Andrew as quickly as I could.'

'Forget about it; I survived. Now drink your coffee.'

'Yes, sir!'

He smiled, but as she drank the coffee obediently his expression darkened slightly. Unwillingly he found himself looking back over his life. How many of the people he had worked with would have abandoned everything to rush to his bedside if he had been hurt? He supposed his father might have dragged himself away from his practice if it hadn't been too busy, but his friends. . .? It was a strangely depressing thought.

'Sorry—what did you say?' he said in confusion, suddenly aware that Bridie was gazing expectantly at him.

'I only asked if you had any problems with the surgery,' she declared. 'Me throwing you in at the deep end like that.'

Jack shook his head. 'Fiona and I coped magnificently. I didn't do anything radical—just stitched up a few minor cuts, wrote a couple of sick lines, renewed some prescriptions—oh, and I prescribed some tranquillisers for John Harvey.'

She put down her coffee. 'You did what?' Her voice was quiet, even.

'I noticed you'd been prescribing iron for him, but I'd say he was suffering from depression rather than anaemia.'

'So you changed the prescription—just like that?'

A slight feeling of unease crept over him. Her face had set into a rigid, cold mask.

'I didn't think you'd mind,' he continued a little uncertainly. 'I thought—'

'You thought—*you* thought!' she exploded. 'Just who the hell do you think you are—coming in for one surgery and altering the medication I'd prescribed?'

'It was two surgeries, to be exact.' He smiled winningly. 'And it's really no big deal, Bridie. You've had him on a course of iron for the last two months, and as it didn't seem to be helping him at all I decided that his problem was probably psychological, so tranquillisers would be the best prescription—'

'I don't give a damn if it *is* the best option,' she threw at him. 'I don't give a damn if tranquillisers have suddenly become the elixir of life; Mr Harvey is *my* patient; the iron I prescribed was what *I* considered was best for his condition. If nothing else I would have thought common professional courtesy would have urged you to discuss any alteration to his treatment with me before just going ahead and doing it!'

'All I did was make a clinical judgement based on my not inconsiderable experience—'

She got to her feet quickly, knocking over the remnants of her coffee in her anger. 'All you did, Dr

Culrain, was completely undermine my patient's confidence in me!'

He flushed deeply. 'Bridie—'

'Listen to me, and listen good,' she interrupted, her eyes blazing. 'If you ever—*ever*—interfere with one of my patients again, if you ever just go ahead and alter my prescription because *you* decide it would be for the best I'll make you wish you'd never been born. Do you understand me?'

If he'd had time to consider her reaction, if her reprimand had been delivered in private instead of in front of others he would have acknowledged that he would have reacted in exactly the same way if someone had countermanded *his* instructions. But he did not have time to think and they were not alone.

All too clearly he could hear sniggers emanating from the table of junior doctors behind him, and that, coupled with the knowledge that he had not only behaved like a fool but was being seen to be one, fuelled rather than dampened his anger.

'No one—*no one*—has ever questioned my professional integrity before!' he said furiously, his colour high.

'Then it's obviously high time someone did!' she retorted.

He took one step forward, torn between a quite irrational desire either to shake the living daylights out of her or kiss her ruthlessly, and to his surprise Bridie didn't move an inch. She just stared at him with cold anger, totally in control of herself.

'If you intend working with me, Dr Culrain, then I expect some common professional courtesy from you. If you can't accord me that, then I think we'd better part company right here and now. It's your decision and, unlike you, I'll give you time to think about it. I'll expect your decision when you get back to the house.'

And with that she turned on her heel and walked away from him.

He stood for a moment, uncertain whether he should go after her, and then whirled round as he heard the sound of laughter behind him.

'One of you has something you'd like to add?' he demanded, staring at the table of doctors, his eyes narrowed, his face white.

The laughter died, heads were swiftly averted, and quickly the doctors made their escape—all except one, who lingered by the doorway.

'That was some performance,' the doctor observed. 'I'm Neil, by the way, Neil Jardine.'

'I'm glad you enjoyed it, Neil,' Jack replied tersely.

'She shouldn't have spoken to you like that.'

Jack sighed and then shook his head ruefully. 'She had some justification.'

'Perhaps—but don't you think it might have been better for her to have waited until later, when you were both alone?'

'I fail to see why Dr McEwen should have to explain her actions to anyone, least of all you,' Jack retorted.

Neil regarded him curiously, and Jack could understand his puzzlement. A minute or two ago he could cheerfully have strangled Bridie, and yet now here he was, rushing to her defence. It made no sense at all.

A flicker of understanding appeared on Neil's face. 'So that's your game plan, is it? Do you think it will work?'

'My game plan?'

'With Bridie—our ice maiden. It's a novel idea, taking all she dishes out and hoping she'll melt. No one's tried that method before—and, believe me, we've all had a shot at her. The hospital's been running a sweepstake for years on the odds on anyone getting her into bed, but no one's even got to first base.'

'Could the problem be that Dr McEwen has some taste?' Jack asked, conscious of a sudden and quite irrational surge of dislike towards the blond Adonis who stood before him.

'You've got the best opportunity anyone's ever had—living in the same house, with old Andrew safely out of the way—'

'He's been in a car crash, for God's sake!' Jack snapped.

'And we're all very sorry,' Neil Jardine replied quickly, 'but he's going to recover, and until then you've got a golden opportunity—'

'And you're going to require some quite extensive dentistry if you don't get out of my sight right now!'

Neil took one look at Jack's furious face and went.

Jack glared at the closed canteen door for a second and then groaned out loud. What the hell was he doing? He had almost come to blows with a man he didn't know over a woman he didn't, at this moment, particularly like.

What did it matter if the junior doctors had given Bridie a nickname? It was nothing to do with him, and yet he had felt quite irrationally angry, and protective—yes, that was the word, he thought with amazement, protective. Towards her—the woman who had humiliated him in public.

He had never felt like this before and he didn't like it one bit. It suggested something he had steered clear of all his life—involvement.

Absently he mopped up the coffee she had spilt. He supposed he could always leave—she had given him that ultimatum—but he knew he wouldn't. He'd promised Andrew that he would fill in for him, and running out on a job was not his style. He shook his head wryly. One thing was sure—he was going to have to be careful from now on when it came to Bridie McEwen.

Bridie had scarcely drawn her car to a halt outside Andrew's large Victorian house when Fiona rushed down the steps towards her, her face anxious.

'If you'd been another five minutes I was coming to the hospital myself! How is Andrew?'

Bridie told her.

'The telephone's never stopped ringing since you left, with people enquiring about him,' Fiona declared, torn between pride and fatigue. 'Thank God he's going to be all right, but how on earth are you going to manage? Could Jack stay on as locum for longer than just three weeks, do you suppose? Where is he, by the way?' she added, peering past Bridie into the night.

'In Timbuktu for all I care.'

Fiona raised her eyes heavenwards and followed her into the house.

'Thanks for staying on,' Bridie continued as she put her medical bag down on the hall table. 'I really appreciate it, but you get off home now. I'm for a long, hot bath—' She came to a halt with a sigh as Fiona shook her head at her apologetically. 'Don't tell me—an emergency call's come in.'

'Afraid so. Jamie Dunn's mother phoned just a minute ago—he's having a bad asthma attack. I was just going to contact Dr Maxwell out at Pitagowan to see if he could cover for you.'

Wearily Bridie picked up her bag again and went back outside, just as the roar of an exhaust heralded Jack's approach.

'Something wrong?' he asked as he got out of his car.

'An emergency.'

'I'll cover it.'

'I think you've done more than enough for one day already.'

The irony in her voice was unmistakable, but not a muscle moved on his face. 'You're just about dead on your feet,' he replied evenly. 'I'll take the call.'

Deliberately she got into her car, but when she tried to close the door she found it caught and held in a vice-like grip.

'There's being dedicated, Bridie, and there's being a bloody fool. And right now you're behaving like a bloody fool,' he said, his voice infuriatingly calm. 'If you insist on this madness then I insist on driving you—the last thing I need is you ending up in a hospital bed next to Andrew.'

For a second she considered arguing with him and then dismissed it. She *was* tired, and tired doctors made mistakes. Without a word she got out of the car and into the passenger seat.

'Directions to our patient, please,' he said, fastening his seat belt.

She gave them, and then said nothing more during the short drive to Jamie Dunn's home, despite Jack's occasional sidelong glance. It was petty—childish, even—to behave that way, but she didn't care. He had questioned her medical judgement and she wasn't going to forgive him that in a hurry.

They could hear Jamie's high-pitched cries even from outside the house, and Bridie's heart sank. A hysterical seven-year-old child was hard enough to deal with, but a hysterical seven-year-old with asthma was a nightmare.

'Good pair of lungs,' Jack observed as they walked up to the house.

'I only wish they were,' she replied. 'Jamie suffers from chronic asthma,' she added as his eyebrows rose questioningly.

Mrs Dunn was clearly terrified, and in her fear she was doing the worst possible thing—holding Jamie tight. She was, of course, simply trying to comfort him, but her well-intentioned action was only constricting his breathing even more. Gently Bridie attempted to prise Jamie away, but he simply screamed even louder and clung to his mother.

'I'm so sorry, Doctor,' Mrs Dunn declared, her eyes large with fear. 'He forgot to use his inhaler—I've tried to impress on him how important it is—but he forgot and—'

'It's all right, Mrs Dunn,' Bridie said soothingly. 'Jamie, I'm just going to put this mask over your face and I want you to try and breathe as deeply as you can for me.'

Jamie kicked out at her in panic, sending the face-mask and nebuliser spinning out of her hands. His colour was getting higher and higher, his breathing was coming in great, ragged gasps, and Bridie bit her lip. Somehow she had to get him to use the nebuliser—if she couldn't then they were going to have a major emergency on their hands.

'Is this your football, Jamie?' Jack asked, picking it up. 'I used to play a bit when I was younger. Had a try-out for Manchester United, but then I got the medical bug and decided to swap my football for a stethoscope.'

Jamie's sobs continued, but he pulled a little away from his mother to stare at this stranger.

'I'm just back from Italy,' Jack continued. 'Now, there's a wonderful place for the real football fan. I used to watch AC Milan play every week and I'll tell you something—those continental players could certainly teach the British footballers a thing or two.'

'They're. . .they're rubbish!' Jamie gasped.

'Now, how can you say that?' Jack demanded,

slipping the face-mask deftly over the child's head. 'Granted, they might not have the defensive players Britain has, but when it comes to strikers—well, there's no competition.'

Jamie shook his head deliberately.

'Deep breaths now, Jamie.' Jack smiled. 'You know, you'd be amazed at how many professional footballers suffer from asthma; mind you, they're sensible—they remember to use their inhalers and you better had too if you want to play for England.'

'Scotland!' Jamie wheezed, with a look of profound disgust. 'I want to play for Scotland!'

Already his breathing was slightly easier, his colour not so high. Bridie glanced across at Jack. She had to hand it to him. He'd done an excellent job.

'Will he have to go to hospital?' Mrs Dunn asked, torn between relief and anxiety.

'I think it would be wise—just for the night,' Bridie said gently, taking her cellphone from her bag and beginning to dial. 'After a few hours on a drip he'll be right as rain.'

'Thank you, Doctor; oh, *thank you*!' Mrs Dunn exclaimed.

'Don't thank me—thank Dr Culrain,' she replied, and to Jack's surprise there was no irony in her voice. He stared at her and she smiled slightly. 'I always give credit where credit's due, Jack.'

They waited until the ambulance arrived, Jamie still arguing with Jack about the relative merits of various football players, and then headed back to her car.

'Tell me something,' she said as she opened her car door. 'Was any of that true—what you told Jamie about trying out for Manchester United and watching AC Milan play every week?'

'Not a word.' He grinned.

'So you're a good liar too—I'll have to remember that.'

'I don't make a habit of it, I can assure you,' he replied, wondering why her voice sounded suddenly so hard. 'My tall tales are reserved solely for terrified small boys. Now, I think we'd better start making tracks,' he added as she leant against the car wearily.

'In a minute. It's such a lovely night.'

She was right, Jack thought as he breathed in deeply. He had been abroad for so long that he had forgotten evenings like this, when the air was sweet and warm with the scent of honeysuckle and the sky bright with a scattering of stars.

He turned to agree with her and caught his breath sharply. She had tilted her head slightly to look at the moon, and the slight night-time breeze that was rustling through the honeysuckle in Mrs Dunn's garden was also teasing tendrils of chestnut hair from the confines of her chignon, sending them curling and stroking across her forehead and neck.

Such an overwhelming feeling of desire flooded through him that he pulled open the driver's door fiercely.

'Time to go, Bridie.'

She nodded.

They drove back to the house in silence, both lost in their own thoughts, but when they got out of the car she paused for a moment. 'I gave you an ultimatum back at the hospital. Have you decided whether you'll be staying on at the practice until I can find a replacement, or—?'

'I would like to stay, if you'll let me.'

'You did a good job tonight,' she murmured, wishing that she could see his face, but it was in shadow. 'If you're prepared to stay on then I'm prepared to agree to having you.'

'Does that mean I'm forgiven for Mr Harvey and the tranquillisers?'

'Don't push your luck, Jack,' she said drily.

She heard his deep chuckle in the dark and smiled. He was completely impossible, but he was oh, so likeable. She didn't know how on earth they were going to work together, but work together they must.

All she could hope was that she could find a replacement for him before he turned her whole world upside down.

CHAPTER THREE

'GOD, how I hate Monday mornings.'

'You hate *all* mornings, Fiona!' Bridie chuckled as she switched on the kettle. 'Think positive—with luck we might have a light surgery today.'

'No, we won't,' Fiona replied gloomily. 'We'll have a mob in; we always do on a Monday. Makes you wonder what folk get up to at the weekend, doesn't it?'

'My, but we're a little ray of sunshine this morning, aren't we?' Bridie laughed. 'What's up? Something wrong with Robert or the kids?'

'No, nothing. I'm just suffering from a bad attack of the glooms, I guess. Jack still in bed?'

Bridie nodded as she spooned some coffee into two cups.

'I thought he was supposed to be doing all the morning surgeries?' Fiona observed.

'I like to do the occasional one.'

'What you mean is you don't trust him.'

'Of course I trust him,' Bridie declared, her cheeks flushing slightly. 'Do you want a biscuit to go with your coffee? I've shortbread, oat crunchies, and there's some chocolate ones. . .' She came to a halt, aware that her receptionist was shaking her head at her. 'I *do* trust him, Fiona; I just like to know what's going on, that's all.'

'So you're getting on well with him, are you?'

'We're getting on fine,' Bridie replied lightly.

'So what's with this, then?' Fiona asked, stretching up to pull a neatly typed sheet of paper from one of the cupboard doors. 'If my eyes don't deceive me it's a kitchen rota—that really shows how well you're getting on, doesn't it? And don't think I haven't noticed how you've engineered the duty rosters too,' she continued as Bridie tried to interrupt. 'You know what you're doing, don't you? You're doing your level best to ensure you see as little of him as possible!'

'That's not true—'

'No?'

'I can't help it if we've been really busy over the last two weeks.'

Fiona sighed as she took the cup of coffee from her. 'Bridie, this is me you're talking to, not Andrew. Jack's a nice bloke; he likes you, and you like him—I know you do. Can't you just relax a little, give a little, and see what happens?'

'You know I can't.' Bridie's voice was muffled, strained.

'Not all men are like Cameron,' Fiona said gently, and Bridie bit her lip.

'I wish I'd never told you about him.'

'You wouldn't have if we both hadn't got very drunk that night. I'd had a row with Robert and you'd just arrived in Struan and we were both feeling a bit down. I'm glad you told me, and I'm sure if you told Jack he'd understand.'

Bridie shook her head deliberately.

'Bottling up something like that isn't the answer, Bridie.'

'You mean I should shout it from the roof-tops—Dr McEwen was raped by her best friend's father when she was twelve?' Bridie said bitterly.

'No, of course I don't mean that,' Fiona exclaimed. 'But it wasn't your fault. It was never your fault.'

Bridie stared down into her coffee blindly. 'I know,' she said with difficulty. 'God, I should do—I had enough people telling me that when I had therapy.'

'Then why won't you believe it? Why can't you tell Jack?'

'How can I?' Bridie said, her eyes bleak. 'Do you know how long it took me to learn to trust a man, to feel comfortable going out with one, let alone have one touch me? I was twenty-three when I met Cameron, and I only told him because I thought he loved me—and the look in his eyes. . . He was horrified, Fiona, disgusted.'

'That was his problem.'

'Was it?' Bridie said ironically. 'He said he still loved me despite everything; he said he could show me what love was like—and it was a nightmare, Fiona. No matter what he did, no matter how hard he tried I just couldn't. . .I just froze. Sometimes I think Cameron was right, that I am frigid.'

Fiona got to her feet quickly, her eyes angry. 'Don't you ever let me hear you say that again—do you hear me? There is *nothing* wrong with you! You had a hellish experience when you were young and of course you're frightened—who wouldn't be?—and the last thing you needed was some insensitive clot coming into your life.

'There is no such thing as a frigid woman, Bridie—you, as a doctor, should know that. There are only inadequate men who are so selfish, so intent on satisfying their own desires that they couldn't arouse an *experienced* woman, far less someone who's been through what you have!'

'Perhaps.'

'Perhaps nothing! You know what I'm saying is true.'

'We'd better get this surgery started,' Bridie declared, rinsing her mug in the sink.

'Bridie—'

'Look, it's my problem. Thanks for listening, but it's my problem—and I want it to stay that way, Fiona.'

'What do you take me for?' her receptionist demanded. 'I won't say a word to anyone—I never would.'

Bridie hugged her tightly. 'Thanks. Now we'd better get this show on the road.'

The surgery was a busy one, as Fiona had predicted, but Bridie didn't care. She loved her work. It was challenging and fulfilling, and it was a refuge from her past. When she worked she thought of nothing but the patients who sat in front of her. Their worries and fears took precedence over everything else. She never begrudged the time she spent with her patients—well, hardly ever. There was one who stretched her compassion and understanding to the limit.

'Last one coming up, Bridie,' Fiona declared, popping her head round the consulting room door just as the surgery clock struck eleven o'clock.

'Who is it?'

'Can't you guess?'

Bridie sighed. 'Send her in.'

Mrs Findlay's eyes registered obvious disappointment as she sat down heavily. 'I was really rather hoping to see Dr Culrain, Dr McEwen.'

'I'm afraid Dr Culrain's not on duty this morning, Mrs Findlay,' Bridie said smoothly. 'You'll just have to settle for me.'

'I don't mean to give offence, my dear,' Mrs Findlay explained, permitting her plump and placid face to crease into the semblance of a smile, 'but, you see, Dr Culrain really seems to *understand* my condition. I wonder—might it be better if I came back tomorrow, when Dr Culrain's here?'

Bridie was tempted. It had been a long surgery, and she still had the rounds to do. The odds were that there was absolutely nothing wrong with Mrs Findlay—the woman virtually made a profession out of imaginary ailments—but she knew she couldn't risk it. There was always the chance that this time there might actually be something wrong with her.

'As you're already here, Mrs Findlay, I might as well check you out,' she said with more enthusiasm than she felt. 'If you'd just slip behind the screens and get undressed, I'll be with you in a minute.'

As Mrs Findlay did as she asked Bridie sat at her desk, lost in thought. It was remarkable how quickly Jack had become accepted in the area. Rural Scottish communities were notorious for regarding incomers with deep suspicion, deliberately keeping their distance until they had decided whether you were a person to be trusted or not, but it hadn't been like that with Jack.

No matter where she went she heard nothing but praise for him—and it wasn't just from the women, she thought wryly. Even old Mr Brownlie, who had given her the rough edge of his tongue for almost two years before finally accepting her, had fallen completely under Jack's spell.

'I'm ready now, Doctor.'

Bridie sighed and got to her feet. She just didn't understand it; she just didn't understand it at all.

'Well, everything seems to be in perfect order, Mrs Findlay,' she said some time later as she put away her stethoscope.

Mrs Findlay looked distinctly aggrieved. 'I can't see how that's possible, Doctor, when I don't seem to have any appetite at all. Do you think my lack of appetite could be due to the complaint Dr Culrain is certain I'm suffering from?'

Bridie looked up quickly from the notes she was making. 'What complaint would that be?'

'Dr Culrain spotted it almost immediately—not last

Monday, when I came in to see him about my heart murmur, but last Thursday, when I was showing him my bad leg and wondering whether it was due to phlebitis,' Mrs Findlay declared. 'He said that in his medical opinion I was almost certainly suffering from morbidity neurosis—in fact he said mine was about the worst case he had ever come across.'

'Oh, dear,' Bridie declared solemnly, only just choking down the laughter that threatened to overwhelm her. 'And did Dr Culrain think he could cure you?'

'Apparently some people suffer from it all their lives, and Dr Culrain rather feared I might be one of them,' Mrs Findlay sighed, with no small degree of satisfaction. 'It's not life-threatening, you understand, just debil—delib—'

'Debilitating?'

'That's it. Dr Culrain suggested the environment round here might be worsening my condition, so I was wondering whether you thought a short stay with my daughter in Inverness might be the answer?'

'I think that's an excellent idea,' Bridie replied with difficulty as she opened the consulting-room door.

'You know, you mustn't take it too much to heart that you didn't spot what was wrong, my dear,' Mrs Findlay commented as she stood in the hallway. 'Dr Culrain told me that absolutely no blame could be attached to you or to Dr Weston. He only recognised my condition because he's worked abroad so extensively.'

Bridie only just contained herself, and as soon as the front door had closed safely behind Mrs Findlay she ran up to the sitting room quickly.

'Something wrong?' Jack asked, glancing up from his newspaper.

'You are incorrigible!' she gasped.

'What have I done now?'

She burst out laughing. 'Mrs Findlay and her morbidity neurosis—oh, Jack, you told her she was a hypochondriac!'

'And so she is,' he declared.

'I know, but what if she looks up morbidity neurosis in a dictionary?'

'With any luck she'll be none the wiser, and if she is—so be it.'

'You really shouldn't have done it,' she said, trying to look severe and failing miserably. 'She's going off to Inverness to stay with her daughter in the hope that a change of scene will ease her condition.'

'Hallelujah—there is a God!'

'But it's not very ethical, Jack—'

'You can't tell me you haven't been wishing for a temporary respite from that woman for years,' he declared. 'Well, I've got you one, so don't knock it.'

She shook her head and laughed again. 'You're impossible—but thank you. I'm off on my rounds now. See you later.'

'Why don't I come with you?'

She paused at the door.

'Look, Bridie, the sooner I find my way around, the sooner this is going to become a more efficient practice. Right now all I'm doing is sitting about once I've finished the surgeries, while you take the visiting rounds and share the night-time emergencies with Bob Maxwell at Pitagowan. It doesn't make sense.'

He was right; she knew he was.

'Perhaps tomorrow, Jack. I'm running behind today as it is, and I really don't have time to wait until you're ready to go.'

He pulled his medical bag out from under the kitchen table. 'I'm ready.'

'But I'm going to have lunch out on the road, and

I've only made enough sandwiches for one.'

He pocketed an apple from the fruit bowl. 'I could do with losing some weight.'

She stared at him indecisively and his lips curved into a wicked grin.

'Good Lord—don't tell me you've run out of excuses already, Bridie?'

She struggled with herself for a moment, and then started to laugh. 'I just can't win, can I?' she said.

'I didn't realise we were in competition,' he replied.

She opened her mouth and then shut it again. That was exactly how she felt, she thought wryly—as though she was locked into a competition with him—a competition she invariably lost. It wasn't just his very definite masculinity that was so unsettling, it was his unerring ability to cap everything she said, his ability to reduce her to silence.

'Come on, then,' she declared. 'Let me show you the joys of Perth-shire.'

It was a beautiful August day, the clouds nothing more than thin ribbons of white in an otherwise clear blue sky. The ripening fields shone like burnished gold and even Struan's grey houses took on a kind of beauty, their hard edges softened by the warm glow of summer. In the distance a slight heat haze hung shimmering over the hills, and Bridie rolled down her window. It was going to be hot.

'Now, the best way to find your way about here is to forget about traditional things like signposts and rely instead on specific landmarks,' she declared as they left Struan behind them. 'Most houses and farms are named after geographical features—Black Hill Farm, Ash Tree Cottage, Struan Heights—so look out for cairns, hills, clumps of trees, that sort of thing.'

'You mean those indistinct blurs that keep passing the windscreen?'

She glanced across at him. 'Are you attempting to suggest—not very subtly, I might add—that I'm driving too fast?'

'When I've found the courage to prise my fingers off the dashboard I'll let you know,' he replied.

'Oh, come on, I'm not driving that fast!' she protested.

'Doing seventy on a road intended for thirty is pretty fast to my way of thinking.'

'Chicken!'

'I'd just like to see my fortieth birthday if it's all the same to you,' he observed.

'OK, OK,' she chuckled. 'How's this?' she added, slowing down considerably.

'That's more like it.' He smiled. 'Now, who are we calling on first?'

'One of my favourite patients—Elsa Livingstone. She's had a really hard life bringing up two kids on her own after her husband died in an accident, but she never complains. According to her phone call she's burnt her arm a little—but, knowing her, that means it's pretty severe.'

'The stoical type?'

'Too damn stoical. She always thinks she's being a nuisance and she's anything but. Her main fault is waiting too long before she gets help.'

'She's accident-prone, then?'

'This last year she has been. Nothing really serious, you understand, just minor things—but painful none the less.'

He nodded. 'Is this where she lives?' he asked as they bounced down a rough track towards a small whitewashed cottage.

'Yes, this is Heather Cottage.'

'Where's the heather?'

'It's all around you.'

'You mean that brown dead stuff?'

'You *are* a townie, aren't you?' she laughed. 'It doesn't get purple until the end of August or beginning of September.'

'So much for geographical detail helping me to find my way around,' he protested. 'It's not much use if it keeps on changing.'

'Sorry,' she chuckled, 'but I can't do much about that. Oh, there's Mrs Livingstone,' she added as she pulled the car to a halt. 'What have you been up to, Elsa?'

'Just a stupid accident with the frying-pan, Doctor.'

Bridie shook her head. 'Let's take a look at it, then. This is Dr Culrain, Elsa,' she continued, following her into her sitting room. 'He's filling in for Andrew.'

Mrs Livingstone's thin, worn face creased into a warm smile of welcome.

'You know, you really should have got your son to drive you over to the accident and emergency unit at Perth as soon as this happened.' Bridie sighed as she removed the makeshift dressing that Elsa had put on the wound and began cleaning it.

'I ran it under cold water like they say you should, Doctor, and I thought that would be enough. Bill was watching football on the television—you know how he likes his sport—and I didn't want to disturb him, what with him always being so good to me and all.'

Bridie said nothing. It was common knowledge that Mrs Livingstone's son was a lazy scrounger, squeezing every penny he could from his mother, but it was not for her to say so—nor, indeed, would Mrs Livingstone have believed her.

'I want you to come down to the surgery and let me have a look at this in a couple of days,' Bridie declared as she put a sterile dressing on the arm. 'If you feel any discomfort, or if it starts to weep at all, don't wait until Wednesday—come down straight away.'

'I'm sure there'll be no need, Doctor—it feels easier already.'

'Wednesday, Elsa—I want to see you at the surgery on Wednesday,' Bridie said firmly.

'I'll try my best, Doctor, but I can't promise,' Elsa said hesitantly. 'It's the transport problem, you see.'

'Your son has a car, hasn't he?'

'Yes, but he usually takes his friends to Dundee on a Wednesday; they do a bit of shopping and then go on to a club in the evening—you know what young lads are like.'

Bridie clenched her fingers together tightly. At thirty-five Bill Livingstone was scarcely a young lad. He'd had countless jobs—all of them offered by people who liked and respected his mother—and he hadn't been able to hold down one of them. It was appalling that at almost seventy his mother had to continue farming to give them both something to live on. Her daughter, Alice, had done really well, with a good job in banking in Edinburgh, but Bill. . . For two pins Bridie would have given him a piece of her mind if she'd thought it would do any good.

'If Bill can't bring you down on Wednesday I'll drop in myself while I'm out on my rounds, Elsa,' she said. 'It would be no trouble at all,' she added as Mrs Livingstone began to protest. 'It's all part of the job.'

Jack was unusually silent as they drove away from Elsa Livingstone's cottage.

'Something bothering you?' she said at last.

'These accidents of Mrs Livingstone's—you're absolutely certain they *are* accidents?'

She pulled the car to a halt sharply. 'What do you mean?'

'I couldn't help noticing that her legs were pretty bruised. Have you considered the possibility that she might be experiencing the first stages of Alzheimer's disease—getting forgetful and so having accidents?'

She frowned slightly. 'She isn't displaying any of the usual symptoms.'

'Could she be suffering from depression, then—deliberately injuring herself?'

'Oh, no, Jack; I can't believe that!'

'There's another alternative, if these accidents aren't just accidents, and it's not a pleasant one.'

She stared at him in horror. 'You don't mean you think her son—?'

'It happens, Bridie, and all too frequently, I'm afraid,' he commented. 'He could be assaulting her.'

She bit her lip and then nodded slowly. 'I'll keep an eye on the situation, and thanks for the tip.'

He shook his head. 'I just hope I'm wrong.'

'So do I,' she sighed.

The rest of the morning flew quickly by. There was a visit to Rob Wishart to check how his broken leg was mending, a call on the McPhersons to examine the new baby, and it was a little before one o'clock when they finally arrived at the Donaldsons' farm at Cairn Hill.

'From the description Mrs Donaldson gave I'd say one of the triplets has the measles,' Bridie declared as she pulled her medical bag out of the car. 'Unfortunately that means the other two have probably got it as well—the Donaldson triplets never do anything singly.'

'Weren't they vaccinated?'

'I'm afraid the Donaldsons point-blank refuse to allow their children to have any vaccinations,' she replied. 'I've pleaded, I've argued, I've done everything I can think of—but they just won't budge.'

'How old are the children?'

'Two years old—and the cutest bundles of mischief you ever saw.'

Bridie's prophecy was right—all three of the triplets were covered by the classic mottled pink rash.

'There's not a lot I can do now, Mrs Donaldson,' she sighed. 'Didn't you notice they seemed a bit feverish, with runny noses and a little bit of a dry cough?'

'I thought they all just had a cold, Doctor.'

'Melanie's not too bad, but Jodie and Sam both have an ear infection,' Bridie continued. 'I'll treat that with antibiotics, and the spots should start disappearing in a day or two—starting at the face and then working down the rest of their bodies. But they're all highly infectious, so keep them away from other children and definitely away from anyone you know is pregnant.'

Mrs Donaldson nodded.

'Measles isn't a trivial complaint, you know, Mrs Donaldson. I don't want to frighten you but sometimes it can lead to encephalitis—inflammation of the brain. If you'd had them all vaccinated when I suggested, you could have saved them a lot of discomfort.'

'Well, they won't get measles again, Doctor, so that's one less thing for me to worry about,' Mrs Donaldson said complacently.

'But what about the next illness? It could be whooping cough or diphtheria next time,' Bridie said, only just keeping her temper.

'We don't hold with vaccinations, Doctor, you know that. We never have done, have we, Jim?'

Her husband shook his head. 'You hear such dreadful things, Doctor,' he said. 'Children right as rain one day and then brain-damaged the next, after they've been inoculated.'

'There's certainly a slight danger for children who are prone to epileptic fits,' Jack commented smoothly, sensing Bridie's mounting anger, 'but I understand from Dr McEwen that your children are very healthy, so actually there's more chance of them dying from whooping cough than from being injured by the vaccination.'

'Dying?' Mrs Donaldson repeated, fear plain on her face.

Jack nodded, and then proceeded to explain the pros and cons of immunisation, how particular elements could be omitted from the vaccination if there was the least chance of an adverse reaction. He said nothing that Bridie hadn't said at least a hundred times before but, to her disbelief, this time the Donaldsons lapped up every word.

By the time they left the farm Jack had not only persuaded the family of the benefits of immunisation but he had actually got them to sign the children up for a complete course. It was infuriating.

'Nice family, the Donaldsons,' he commented.

'They are,' she said tightly.

'And, like you said, those kids are really cute—spots or no spots.'

'Yes.'

'Something the matter?' he asked curiously, glancing across at her set face.

She pulled the car off the road. 'This looks as good a place as any to have lunch—bring your apple along.' And with that she got out of the car and strode towards a small incline, leaving him to follow her, his face puzzled.

She had already settled herself down in the grass and unwrapped her sandwiches by the time Jack caught up with her.

'Do you want one?' she said evenly. 'I made two and I'm not really that hungry.'

'Look, Bridie, something's clearly eating you,' he

said, sitting down beside her, 'and I'm not a mind-reader—'

'How do you do it?' she demanded angrily. 'I've done everything but kidnap those children to try and persuade their parents to let me vaccinate them, and you waltz in and achieve it in one visit. And it's not just the Donaldsons. Good God, even Mrs Findlay sang your praises this morning, and I would have thought only a combination of Mother Teresa and St Francis of Assisi could have achieved that miracle!'

'Jealous?' he suggested, taking a bite out of the sandwich.

'No—yes, damn it, I am!' she retorted. 'Do you know how long it's taken me to become accepted by this community? Five years—*five years*—and yet in the space of two weeks everyone loves you!'

'Not everyone.'

His eyes were fixed on her and she knew very well what he meant, but she had no intention of going down that particular avenue. 'So what's the secret of your success, then—with the patients?' she asked.

'I'm a man.'

'That's it?' she protested.

'I'm afraid so. It might be almost the twenty-first century but there's still a lot of people who think unless you're masculine you're not a proper doctor.'

'Well, I point-blank refuse to have a sex change,' she exclaimed. 'So what do you think of the countryside round here?' she continued hurriedly as his eyes gleamed and she knew without doubt that he was about to make some personal observation.

'The countryside?' he answered gravely. 'Let me see now—lots of fields of wheat—'

'Barley, actually.'

'OK—lots of fields of barley, a very rugged terrain with some high mountains and the occasional lake—'

'Loch.'

He grinned. 'Sorry, *loch*. What else? An inordinate amount of sheep, some cattle, and the occasional sign of human habitation.'

'We call that a house.'

'Ouch!' He laughed. 'I'm a city man, Bridie—Vancouver, Paris, Milan—'

'You don't like it here?'

'That's too strong. It's just. . .different, I guess.'

'I wouldn't like to keep moving from practice to practice the way you do,' she observed, taking the half of apple he offered. 'I'd never feel as though I belonged; I'd always feel transitory.'

'Which is what I like—the fact that no one knows you. You can live your own life without being under constant scrutiny.'

'But don't you miss the continuity—seeing the same patients over a period of years?'

'Patients like Mrs Findlay, you mean?' he replied, his eyebrows rising comically.

She chuckled. 'No, not like Mrs Findlay. The other ones—the ones you grow to like. You see them through the bad times and the good times—'

'And end up trapped by emotional ties.'

'Is that how you feel?' she said, staring at him curiously. 'That if you get too involved with your patients you're trapped?'

'Commitment's not one of my strong points, if that's what you mean,' he said, throwing his apple core into the distance.

'Why? No, I'm sorry, don't answer that,' she added quickly. 'It's none of my business.'

He half smiled. 'Let's just say I discovered at a very young age that there's no such thing in life as a free lunch. Friends, family, colleagues—they all expect some kind of pay-back eventually.'

'That's a bit cynical, isn't it?' she observed.

'I'd call it realistic,' he replied, his lips twisting slightly. 'My parents hated one another's guts, but divorce would have meant breaking up a very lucrative practice, so they tore one another apart for years—using me as their prime weapon. I never knew from one school holiday to the next whether I'd be showered with presents when I came home or completely ignored.'

'I'm sorry.'

'Don't be,' he said with a short, humourless laugh. 'That kind of family background taught me a very valuable lesson—that the best motto in life is to depend on no one, trust no one but think only of yourself—that way you survive.'

'But when you grew up, left home, you must have had friends, surely?' she pressed.

Jack shrugged. 'As I said before, no one does anything for nothing in this life.'

He lay back in the grass, his hands behind his head, his face shuttered. She stared down at him in confusion. She had thought him confident, assured, but there was a wealth of pain inside the man beside her—pain she could sympathise with. In his own way, she thought with surprise, he was as emotionally crippled as she was.

'Don't go to sleep on me,' she said teasingly as he closed his eyes. 'We have to be back in Struan soon.'

'You're a slave-driver, do you know that, Bridie McEwen?' He yawned. 'Surely we can enjoy the sun for fifteen minutes?'

She sighed. 'OK, fifteen minutes—but no more.'

She slipped off her jacket and lay down in the grass a little way from him. It was so peaceful here—the swifts and swallows wheeling and diving in the sky, the song of a thrush somewhere in the trees behind them. With the warm sun on her face the rest of the world seemed a million miles away.

'Twenty-four.'

She opened her eyes quickly to find him lying on his side beside her, his head propped up on his hand, gazing down at her.

'That's how old you look,' he continued as he saw her puzzled expression. 'Twenty-four.'

'Don't I wish?' she chuckled. 'Almost thirty, I'm afraid.'

'A mere child compared to me.' He smiled.

She smiled back and suddenly their eyes locked, hers uncertain, his asking a question, and then slowly, very slowly he reached out and traced the outlines of her face with his fingertips.

She shivered slightly but she didn't pull away, and when his lips sought hers all she was aware of was the exquisite shudder of pleasure that ran through her body. Instinctively she returned his kiss, revelling in the soft moistness of his lips, the gentle exploration of his tongue.

She could feel the hard muscles of his chest against hers, but all she knew was that she wanted him closer, closer. Never had she felt this way before—as though all her nerve-endings were raw and exposed and longing for his touch—but as her blouse came adrift from her skirt and his hands reached for the soft lace that covered her breasts a cold wave of revulsion swept over her.

Unbidden and unwanted, thoughts of another man's hands, another man's lips rushed to her mind, and fear flooded through her—blind, desperate fear—and she pushed Jack away in panic and struggled to her feet.

'Bridie—'

'Leave. . .me alone!' she gasped, struggling to push her blouse back into her skirt.

'What is it—what's wrong?' he demanded, catching her shoulder gently.

She threw off his hand. 'Don't. . .touch me; I don't want to be. . .touched!'

Her face was chalk-white, her eyes huge with strain, and he moved towards her quickly, only to stop when she backed away from him.

'What just happened—it was a mistake,' she continued, clearly fighting to regain her self-control. 'It will never happen again—do you understand me? I'm going back to the car now. Will you collect the wrappers—for the sandwiches—we mustn't leave litter—'

'Damn the litter, Bridie! Tell me what's wrong, why you're so—'

'You made a mistake, Jack, that's all there is to it,' she said with a coldness that amazed him. 'I don't want to discuss what happened—not now, not ever,' she added as he made to speak. 'If we're going to continue working together it's best we pretend this never happened.'

'Bridie!'

But it was too late. She had picked up her jacket and gone.

CHAPTER FOUR

'BUT I assumed you'd be coming home when you were discharged from hospital, Andrew.'

'Then you assumed wrong, my dear,' he replied. 'Now, could you push me over to one of those tables with an umbrella? We're holding up the traffic.'

Bridie glanced round apologetically at the other patients and their relatives who were attempting to get past them, and then manoeuvred Andrew's wheelchair off the gravel path and onto the lawn in front of the hospital.

'You know, the gardener keeps these grounds quite beautifully,' he continued admiringly. 'There's not a weed to be seen in any of the flower-beds.'

'But why, Andrew?'

'I expect the gardener comes in to weed every day.'

'Oh, Andrew, that's not what I meant and you know it!' she protested.

A faint smile appeared on his deeply lined face for a moment and then he sighed. 'Look at the state of me, Bridie. How is coming home a practical option?'

'So you're in a wheelchair,' she said briskly, pulling over a seat and sitting down beside him. 'It's only temporary, and once your casts are off—'

'And until then? Think about it rationally, my dear. That old house of mine is full of stairs and narrow corridors—it would be impossible.'

'I'll help you, you know that.'

He shook his head. 'Play nursemaid and nanny as well as doctor? You'd be on your knees in a week.'

'It only needs a little adjustment, that's all,' she

insisted. 'Jack will help me; I'm sure he will. I'll work out a rota—'

'Another one?'

A deep flush appeared on her cheeks and her face set. 'So Jack's been talking to you, has he?'

'He drops in for a chat occasionally.'

'And spends the whole time complaining about me, it would appear!'

Andrew thrust his hand through his shock of white hair, irritation plain on his face. 'No, he does not complain about you—ever—so you can come down off your high horse right now, my girl. The matter of the kitchen rota just happened to slip out one day—'

'Oh, I'll bet it did!'

He bit his lip. 'Look, I'm not going to argue with you, Bridie. My sister lives in a bungalow and she's only recently retired from nursing. It makes sense for me to convalesce with her until I'm fully fit and that's exactly what I intend to do.'

She stared out at the hospital grounds. For the last three days she and Jack had been skirting warily round one another, neither of them saying anything, but both aware of the tension that existed between them. The one thing that had kept her going was the thought that Andrew would be coming home soon, that his calming presence would act as a buffer between them, easing the situation, and now it wasn't going to happen.

'I don't see why you're making such a fuss about where I go when I leave hospital anyway,' Andrew observed, breaking into her thoughts. 'From what I've heard Jack seems to have taken to the area like a duck to water. He's only got lost twice—'

'Three times.'

'OK, three times—' he smiled '—but considering he's an incomer that's pretty damn amazing.'

'That's not the point, Andrew—'

'Then what is?' he demanded.

He was waiting for an answer and she gazed at him hopelessly. How could she tell him that she was frightened—frightened of the feelings Jack awoke in her, the feelings that so mocked and humiliated her, for she knew they would never be fulfilled?

'I'm not. . . It's just. . .I suppose I've just got used to working with you,' she said lamely.

'Good grief, Bridie, anyone would think we'd worked together for *twenty*-five years instead of five,' he laughed. 'You and Jack get on well together, don't you?'

'He's a good doctor,' she said evasively.

'And he likes you—'

'Does he?' she broke in, despising herself for her question and yet longing to know, nevertheless.

Andrew gazed at her in surprise. 'Of course he does, and as you haven't kicked him out I thought the liking must be mutual.'

'You make me sound like some kind of harridan,' she murmured uncomfortably.

'Oh, Bridie,' he said, reaching out to take one of her hands in his, 'you're anything but a harridan. It's just that sometimes you make life so difficult for yourself. If only you'd let people see the side of you that I see.'

'You mean the side that's even more bad-tempered and crotchety?' she said, her smile unsteady. 'I don't think the world is ready for that yet.'

He shook his head. 'Bridie, Bridie, what am I going to do with you?'

'Get well and come back to work soon, I hope.'

He let go of her hand and examined the table-top for a moment. 'Actually, it's been crossing my mind just lately that perhaps it's time I started thinking about hanging up my stethoscope.'

'You've a good few years of medicine ahead of you yet, Andrew,' she declared dismissively.

'Perhaps.'

She stared at him uneasily. 'You're not seriously thinking of retiring, are you?'

'I'll have to eventually, and—well—don't you think someone like Jack would be ideal to fill my shoes?'

'*What*?'

'The patients like him, and you said yourself that he's a good doctor. Think how the practice would benefit from the injection of new ideas. You and Jack working together as a team—can't you just picture it?'

She could, all too clearly. 'Andrew, listen to me—'

'Has he told you about the new techniques they're using in Canada for cancer patients?' he continued enthusiastically. 'It's exciting stuff, Bridie. Made me realise that medicine's become a young person's profession, not a job for an old codger like me.'

He wasn't just thinking about retiring, she thought with dismay; he had already made up his mind.

'Andrew, please listen to me—'

'I haven't mentioned the idea to Jack yet,' he said quickly, seeing her look of complete horror, 'so don't go getting all hot and bothered about it. He might not accept—though I have to say I hope he will.'

He point-blank refused to discuss the subject any more, and eventually she left him sitting contentedly in the hospital grounds, her mind in turmoil. It was bad enough that Andrew wasn't coming home, but for him to be actually considering retiring and offering his share of the partnership to Jack!

It was so unfair, she thought angrily as she made her way down to the hospital car park. She had invested five years of her life here and the last thing she wanted was to have to start again somewhere else because of one man—one attractive, unsettling, impossible man. The only comforting thing in this whole mess was her almost absolute certainty that, no matter what Andrew decided or wanted, Jack would never stay on in Struan. He had made his position about staying anywhere for any length of time very clear.

'Hold up a minute, Bridie!'

She turned quickly, forcing a smile to her lips as she recognised the familiar figure running towards her. 'I didn't realise you were on duty today, Simon. How's life treating you?'

'More to the point, how are you?' he asked. He ran his eyes over her critically. 'You're losing weight, my girl, and there wasn't very much of you to start with.'

Self-consciously she pulled the jacket of her suit closer. 'You know what it's like, Simon—in the summer everyone seems to go down with something. We've been inundated with asthma and hay fever sufferers, and there's scarcely a child in the neighbourhood who hasn't got some ailment.'

'But you've had some busy summers before and I've never seen you looking so worn.'

'Age catches up with us all, I guess.' She smiled, beginning to walk on.

He sighed as he followed her. He had seen that shuttered look on her face many times and knew there was no point in pressing her further. 'Has Andrew told you the good news—that we're discharging him this weekend?'

She nodded.

'I thought you'd be over the moon.'

'I'm delighted, of course,' she said with an effort. 'I was just hoping he'd come home to convalesce.'

'Staying with his sister is a sensible idea—'

'Do you know something, Simon? I'm growing heartily sick to death of sensible ideas!' she snapped. 'It was a sensible idea for Jack to stay on at the practice until I found a replacement, and look where that's got me!'

He stopped dead in the middle of the path. 'Has something happened—between you and Jack, I mean?' he demanded.

A faint tinge of colour appeared on her pale cheeks. She would never have said anything at all if her nerves hadn't been stretched wafer-thin, and now she'd landed herself right in it. Simon was like a terrier if he scented any problem where she was concerned.

'Everything's fine,' she said evenly. 'Pay no attention to me. It's this heat—it's making everyone bad-tempered.'

'You're sure that's all it is?'

She gazed up into his frank, open face. He was such a kind man, but even if she hadn't been tortured by memories she knew that she could never have felt anything but friendship for him. Time and time again she'd tried to convince him that she wouldn't change her mind but he just wouldn't give up on her. If only he'd turn his attention to Liz Howard in Men's Surgical. She was really keen on him and he got on so well with her two children, but he just didn't seem to be able to view her in a romantic light.

'You would tell me if there was something wrong, wouldn't you?' he insisted.

'I can safely say you'd be the first to know.' She smiled. 'Now, I really must get on—I'm running late.'

'Are you going to the Struan Agricultural Show on Sunday or are you on duty?' he asked as they reached her car.

'I'm afraid I got the poisoned chalice this year. Andrew should be judging the bonniest baby competition, but as he's not fit I'll have to stand in for him.'

'You have my sympathy!'

'Save it for afterwards when I'll probably need it!' she laughed. 'All I have to do now is arrange emergency cover for the practice.'

'But won't Jack be covering for you?' He frowned.

'Andrew would like him to have the opportunity to go to the show if he wants,' she said as she got into the car.

'Then how about getting Jack to judge the competition?' he suggested maliciously.

'Don't think I haven't been tempted—' she chuckled '—but even I'm not rotten enough to throw him to the lions on his first visit.'

'Any replies yet to your advertisement for a locum?' Simon asked as he closed her car door after her.

She shook her head. 'It's a bit soon yet.'

'Well, a replacement locum can't come soon enough for me,' he said firmly. 'I don't like to see you like this.'

'What—hot and bothered and snappy?' she said, with a laugh that deceived neither of them.

'You know what I mean.'

'Yes, I do,' she said gently, seeing genuine concern in his eyes, 'but please don't worry about me, Simon. I'm fine—honestly.'

She drove out of the hospital driveway quickly, but when she reached the open road she slowed to a tourist crawl. The last place she wanted to go at the moment was home. Jack would be waiting, having extracted a promise from her to spend an hour with him discussing some of their patients, and she did not relish the prospect one bit.

She sighed. If only it wasn't so hot. For the last two weeks the sun had burned relentlessly down from a clear blue sky and still there was no sign of a change. Through her open car windows she could hear the popping sound of melting tar under her wheels, could see that the fields of barley were growing more and more parched.

She eased her jacket off and chuckled wryly as she caught a glimpse of her face in the driving-mirror. God, no wonder Simon had asked if she was all right—she looked dreadful. She wasn't sleeping well but it had nothing to do with work. It was the knowledge that Jack was lying just across the corridor from her, that all she had to do was go and knock on his door.

He wanted her, she knew he did, and she was so attracted to him. When he'd kissed her that day the touch of his lips had sent a fire racing through her body and she had felt herself responding to him. But when his hands had slid under her blouse, when they had travelled to her breasts. . .

She clenched the steering wheel tightly. It did no good to think. Thinking just reminded her that she had been proved inadequate again, just as she had been with Cameron.

All thoughts of Jack disappeared from her mind, however, as she drove down Struan's main street. There was a crowd in the centre of the road—a crowd that parted automatically as she got out of her car.

'I swear to God I didn't see her, Doctor,' a young man declared, grasping hold of her arm urgently, his face white and drawn. 'She just stepped out from nowhere—I tried to brake—'

Bridie glanced past him and saw a car sitting at right angles in the road, and lying in front of it with her schoolbooks scattered round her was Kirsty Ferguson.

'I always said there was going to be an accident on this road one day,' someone muttered. 'Didn't I always say it? These young folk drive through the village as though they were on a motorway.'

Quickly Bridie knelt down beside the teenager. Her

right leg was twisted awkwardly under her, and her hands and arms were badly grazed, but more worrying was the blood pouring from a head wound and the extreme pallor of her skin. Quickly she checked Kirsty's airways for any obstruction and then pulled her stethoscope from her bag.

'I was only doing thirty—I swear I was!' the driver protested, his voice shaking. 'She just came out of nowhere—'

'You were going too fast, lad—I saw you. You must have been doing—'

'Has anyone called for an ambulance?' Bridie interrupted sharply as she applied an absorbent pad to the wound on Kirsty's head.

She didn't like the look of Kirsty one bit. Her pupils were becoming dilated, and her breathing was erratic.

'Mr McDowall at the grocer's called for one as soon as it happened,' a voice from the crowd declared. 'Is she going to be all right, Doctor? Her poor parents—Kirsty's their only child, you know, and they had such a hard time having her.'

Bridie nodded, and then swore under her breath. She'd only looked away for a second and in that time Kirsty's skin had taken on a bluish-grey tinge and her pupils had totally dilated. She'd gone into cardiac arrest.

Quickly she pinched the girl's nose shut and then, taking a deep breath, covered her mouth with her own and blew firmly into her lungs twice. She felt for the carotid pulse in her neck but there was none—none at all.

'Can anyone do CPR—cardiopulmonary resuscitation?' she exclaimed.

There was silence from the crowd, and Bridie's heart sank. Two people working on the girl would have made it much easier, but there was nothing she could do about it.

Swiftly she put the heel of her hand on the lower half of Kirsty's breastbone, locked her other hand over it and began compressing, mentally counting up to fifteen before blowing into the girl's lungs again. On she went and on, compressing for fifteen and then breathing for two, until her shoulders began to ache and her back was screaming in protest.

'You're not going to die, damn you!' she muttered as Kirsty showed no signs of life. 'You are not going to die!'

She could hear the murmurs of sympathy behind her, the whispered sad comments that she was wasting her time, but she refused to stop—she couldn't stop—and then suddenly she was firmly but gently eased aside.

'You do the mouth-to-mouth; I'll do the cardiac compression.' The voice was calm and reassuring.

She nodded. Never had she thought she'd be so pleased to see Jack, but she was.

'Any carotid pulse?' he said.

'None.'

'Pupils?'

'Still dilated.'

'Skin colour?'

'Slightly less blue but not much.'

'OK, let's give it our best shot,' he declared.

They worked as one, Jack compressing Kirsty's chest, Bridie blowing air into her lungs, until, after what felt like an eternity, Bridie felt a pulse. It was faint but it was a pulse.

'I think we've got her, Jack!'

He leant back on his heels and waited, watching, as she continued with the mouth-to-mouth, and when a flush of warm pink colour suddenly suffused Kirsty's ashen cheeks, and she let out a deep sigh, he flashed her a smile that meant more to her than the cheer that went up from the bystanders.

Everything seemed to happen very fast after that. The ambulance arrived, and within minutes Kirsty was being driven out of Struan towards Perth Hospital while the police took statements from the crowd and Jack treated the driver of the car for shock.

'By those skid marks on the road I'd say the poor lad *was* only doing around thirty no matter what everyone else says,' Jack declared as the young man was taken away in the police car and the crowd began to disperse.

'Yes, but a speed limit of thirty miles an hour means that's the maximum you can drive at—not that you should be driving at that all the time,' she replied angrily. 'If only more drivers would lower their speed to twenty in a town more children would live to tell the tale.'

'By "drivers" I suppose you mean everyone else but yourself—and, before you answer that, remember I've driven with you,' he grinned.

'OK, I admit it,' she said ruefully. 'I'm as guilty as the rest, but I'll try not to be in future.'

He walked with her back to her car.

'Do you think she'll be brain-damaged, Jack?' she said uncertainly. 'She wasn't breathing for such a long time.'

'We'll just have to hope she's not. Hey, are you OK?' he added as she shut her eyes tight.

She nodded. 'Just the after-effects—you know how it is.'

He clasped her hand tightly. 'Time you went home.'

His grip was warm, comforting, but instead of feeling strengthened she felt a most ridiculous desire to lean her head on his shoulder and burst into tears.

'I'll see you back at the surgery,' she murmured, getting into her car quickly before her emotions overflowed. 'You want to discuss some patients with me—'

'We can leave it today—'

'I'm fine—just fine. Just give me twenty minutes to have a wash and change my clothes and then I'm all yours.'

He was tempted to say that he only wished she were, but didn't. 'We made a good team today, didn't we?' he said instead.

'Yes—yes, we did.'

Their eyes caught and held for an instant, and then she accelerated and was gone, leaving him to walk back to his car, his face pensive.

With every passing day he knew that he was growing more and more attracted to her, and yet he could not say why. He'd pursued women in the past who were just as intriguing as she was; he'd made love to women who were just as beautiful.

He grimaced slightly. Hell, it wasn't as though she was giving him any encouragement—if anything it was the complete reverse. So was it just that? Was he simply piqued because she kept rejecting him? Was the memory that haunted him of the softness of her body under his hands and the sweetness of her tentative mouth against his only there because she had aroused the hunter in him?

Unconsciously he shook his head. It was more than that and he knew it. When she'd pulled herself free from his arms that day it had been concern he'd felt, not frustration. There had been real fear in her eyes—fear he'd wanted to eradicate by holding her, comforting her. He sighed. It made no sense at all for someone as beautiful as she was to be afraid, unless. . .

A deep furrow appeared between his black eyebrows. A thought had come into his mind—a thought that appalled him—and there was one person who might be able to put his mind at rest.

'Something I can help you with, Jack?' Fiona said, with a smile, glancing up briefly from her typewriter when he appeared at her office door.

'Are you busy?' he said awkwardly.

'You bet. I've a stack of referral letters to do, not to mention this mound of order forms because you and Bridie wait until the last possible minute to tell me we're running out of certain drugs.'

'Sorry,' he said shamefacedly. 'I won't interrupt you, then.'

She nodded and continued with her typing, but he didn't leave. Instead he idly selected case files from the shelves only to replace them, unread. Then he moved to the window and stood for a few moments gazing out, his fingers drumming absently against one of the panes. It was when he finally began to whistle a singularly tuneless song that Fiona finally gave in.

'Look, if there's something you want, Jack, for God's sake, tell me. Otherwise go away and annoy someone else!'

He grinned. 'There is something, but it's a bit personal.'

'You'd better spit it out, then.' She smiled.

'It's about Bridie.'

'What about Bridie?' she said evenly, threading a fresh sheet of paper into her typewriter.

'You're her friend—you probably know her better than just about anyone else round here. Has she ever been married?'

'No.'

'That's it?' he said. 'Just "no"?'

'It's a bit difficult to embroider something like that, Jack. The answer's either yes or no, surely?'

'You could have said she'd been engaged once or

been in a long-term relationship,' he argued.

'But that's not what you asked,' Fiona pointed out. 'You only asked if she'd been married, and the answer's no.'

He shuffled the papers on her desk for a minute. 'Has she. . .was she ever in a violent relationship?'

Fiona's fingers scarcely wavered over her keyboard. 'Why do you ask?'

'You mean she has?'

'I didn't say that, Jack.'

'No, but you don't look shocked by the suggestion, as most people would have done had they known it to be untrue.'

Fiona pulled the ruined sheet of paper from her typewriter and crumpled it into a tight ball. 'Look, Jack, if you want to know anything about Bridie I suggest you ask her, not me. Now, if there's nothing else, I've work to do.'

'Fiona—'

'Sorry I've been so long,' Bridie declared breathlessly as her head came round the office door. 'Let's take a look at the case notes that are bothering you.'

He followed her through to the consulting room. In truth there was only one patient he was concerned about, but for the last week she'd spent so much time avoiding him that this was the only way he could think of for getting her alone.

'Any word of Andrew leaving hospital yet?' he asked as she sat down at the desk.

'He's being discharged on Saturday. Now, these patients—'

'You must be pleased to be having him home.'

'He isn't coming home. He's convalescing with his sister. Now, which patients did you want to discuss with me?'

He gave up. When she was in this mood he knew

that there was no point in trying to get answers—it was like knocking your head against a brick wall.

'This is the last one,' he said some time later. 'John Harvey. He's complaining now of aches and pains in his joints.'

'Arthritis?'

'Could be—' he frowned '—but I'm not happy about these other symptoms he's complained of over the last three months. First it was a flu-type virus that seemed to linger for weeks, then chronic fatigue, and then that bout of depression you hauled me over the coals about when I prescribed tranquillisers. I know none of the symptoms are life-threatening, but it just doesn't feel right somehow.'

Bridie flicked through the case notes in her hand. 'Could we be talking ME here—myalgic encephalomyelitis—or what used to be dismissed as "yuppy flu"?'

'It's possible, I suppose.'

'You're not convinced?'

'Let's just say I've got a gut feeling about this. Would you object if I took some fresh blood samples and arranged for him to have a CAT scan?'

'Go ahead—it can't do any harm.' She got to her feet.

'Bridie, we need to talk.'

'I thought we just had,' she said, gathering up the case notes from her desk. 'But if there's another patient you want to discuss—'

'I want to talk about us.'

'There is no "us",' she said firmly.

'About what happened on Monday. . .' He came to a halt as she gazed back at him, her eyes suddenly large, heather-coloured pools of distress.

'It was a mistake, Jack.'

'I don't agree,' he said quietly.

'I'm sorry about that, but that's the way it is,' she

said, making her way to the consulting room door.

'What, in God's name, did he do to you, Bridie?'

It was a wild shot in the dark, but he saw her back stiffen.

'Who are you talking about?' Her voice was scarcely audible.

'The man who made you so afraid of life, of love.'

For a second she didn't turn round, but when she did her face was cold. 'You're so arrogant, aren't you? So bloody damned arrogant. Just because I don't want to be. . .pawed by you, you immediately assume there has to be a man in it somewhere.'

'Are you telling me there isn't?' he asked, his eyes fixed on her face.

Her lips were dry and she felt sick, but she kept her self-control—just. 'I don't have to tell you anything.'

'Defensive and evasive—doesn't that rather prove my point?'

His voice was gentle, his brown eyes genuinely concerned; it would have been so easy to admit that he was right but she couldn't. Admitting that he had guessed at least part of the truth would have meant being faced with more questions—questions she couldn't and didn't want to answer—and she took refuge in the only form of defence she had—that of attack.

'Spare me the amateur psychology, Jack,' she declared, her tone biting, her eyes furious. 'I've heard it all before, from men whose egos just couldn't stand being rejected, and, believe me, it doesn't improve with the repetition. You made a mistake—a big one. Chalk it up to experience.'

'I can't have so badly misread the situation—'

'You did.' Her voice was a whiplash.

'Bridie, listen—'

'No, *you* listen! How many times do I have to tell you I'm just not interested? What do I have to do or say to make that plain fact penetrate your thick skull? Read my lips, Jack. You made a mistake; I'm not interested—got it?'

She opened the consulting room door and almost collided with Fiona.

'I wasn't eavesdropping—honest,' Fiona said uncomfortably, gazing from Bridie's furious face to Jack's frustrated one. 'I just wanted to tell you that Bob Maxwell phoned when you were out. He said he's more than willing to provide emergency cover if Jack wants to go to the show, but could you let him know one way or the other as soon as possible.'

'What show's this?' Jack asked with an effort, looking at Bridie.

The last thing she wanted was to prolong the conversation. All she wanted was to run to the quiet safety of her room, but she couldn't. Fiona had undoubtedly heard part if not all of their conversation—God, they'd both been shouting loud enough.

'It's the Agricultural Show on Sunday,' she said as evenly as she could. 'I'm going as the judge of the bonniest baby competition in Andrew's place and Andrew wondered whether you'd like to go too.'

He shook his head. 'Thanks for the offer, but sheep and cattle aren't exactly my kind of thing.'

'But it's much more than just a sheep and cattle show,' Fiona protested. 'This is the social event of the year, Jack. There's cake and candy stalls, bric-a-brac, WRI displays, races, tombola.'

His wry expression said it all.

'If Jack doesn't want to go, don't force him,' Bridie said crisply. 'I'll thank Bob for his offer—'

'Simon always goes,' Fiona said innocently.

A slight frown appeared on Jack's forehead. 'Does he?'

Fiona nodded. 'He never misses. He and Bridie usually have a ball.'

The frown deepened. 'I suppose I could drop in—just for a little while.'

'Don't strain yourself!' Bridie retorted tartly, and then flushed as Fiona's eyebrows rose.

'Look, why don't I judge this baby competition thing?' Jack commented thoughtfully. 'I'm Andrew's locum, so logically I should be his replacement. It would give you the whole afternoon to enjoy yourself.'

Bridie shook her head. 'Thanks for the offer, Jack, but judging that particular contest requires a certain skill—'

'Oh, come on, now—how difficult can a baby contest be?' he said scornfully. 'Ten minutes to check the kids over and then I pick one. Anyone with half a brain could do that.'

'But it's not that simple—' Fiona came to an abrupt halt, wincing, as she felt a sharp kick on her shin.

'Jack clearly thinks it is,' Bridie declared sweetly, 'and if he's kind enough to offer then I think we should agree to let him.'

'But Bridie. . .' Fiona began, only to subside into silence at the look she received.

'Good grief, the fuss you women are making anyone would think this was a UN summit,' Jack said airily. 'It's just a few kids lined up for a little local show—I'll do it, no sweat.'

Fiona waited only until he had disappeared up the stairs before she rounded on Bridie. 'That hurt, you know!' she exclaimed, rubbing her shin vigorously.

'I had to shut you up somehow,' Bridie replied, her heather-coloured eyes gleaming.

Fiona shook her head, clearly torn between censure and amusement. 'You really should have warned him, you know.'

'Why? You heard the arrogant devil. Let's see what happens to his overwhelming self-confidence when he's faced with a crowd of irate mums and dads.'

'But they'll crucify him!' Fiona protested.

Bridie's lips twitched and then a peal of laughter came from her. 'I wouldn't be at all surprised!'

CHAPTER FIVE

'YOU'RE not wearing that to the show this afternoon, are you?' Fiona's expression was critical, disparaging.

'What's wrong with it?' Bridie replied, gazing down at her navy blue suit. 'It's smart; it's neat—'

'It's boring.'

'Since when?' Bridie replied defensively. 'You didn't complain when I wore it last year—'

'Then I should have done,' Fiona said frankly. 'Look, Bridie,' she continued, seeing her bristle, 'Struan Agricultural Show is supposed to be a fun day out—a day when you forget you're a doctor and become an ordinary human being like the rest of us. And if that doesn't convince you it's also ninety degrees in the shade out there—you'll melt.'

'I could leave the jacket off, wear a short-sleeved blouse—'

Fiona cast her eyes heavenwards. 'Wow, but we're really talking radical stuff here, aren't we? Wear a dress—and don't tell me you haven't got any,' she added as Bridie opened her mouth. 'I helped you to unpack when you arrived here and I distinctly remember at least two cotton dresses.'

'But that was five years ago,' Bridie protested. 'They'll be well out of fashion now.'

'A dress that's just five years old will be the height of fashion in Struan,' Fiona declared firmly. 'Go on, why not be a little daring? Heaven helps those who help themselves, remember.'

Bridie's eyebrows rose. 'And which Christmas cracker did you get that little homily out of?'

Fiona bounced down the front steps of the house in a huff, and was halfway down the drive before she stopped and turned with clear vexation on her face. 'You know something, Bridie McEwen?' she called. 'There are times when I could cheerfully shake you!'

Bridie curtsied and smiled, which only made her receptionist all the angrier, and then went back into the house, still smiling.

It was strangely silent. Normally it rang to the clatter of Jack's size eleven boots, or to the blare of his radio that he would play at full blast, despite her repeated requests for him to turn it down, but today there was nothing.

A slight frown appeared on her forehead. She'd arranged to travel with him to the show, and if they didn't leave in half an hour they'd have a devil of a job to find a parking space. Bloody man, she thought with irritation. He could never turn up for anything on time.

Idly she wandered into her bedroom and then, on impulse, delved into the deepest recesses of her wardrobe.

There was one dress she'd bought and never worn. It wasn't all that special—just a sun-dress with tiny shoestring straps, a fitted bodice, and a wide skirt that brushed against her calves—but she'd fallen in love with the colour. It was a deep emerald-green, and the shop assistant had gone into raptures when she'd tried it on. Bridie smiled at the memory. The woman had probably just been trying to earn her commission, and anyway the dress probably wouldn't fit now after all these years.

She opened the wardrobe door to put it back and then paused. What harm would it do just to try it on? If it didn't fit there was no point in it cluttering up her wardrobe.

Quickly she pulled off her suit and stepped into the dress. It did fit and it felt wonderfully soft and light. She retrieved a pair of sandals from under her bed and then paused indecisively. Her dressing-table mirror was too small. To see the complete effect she needed a full-length mirror, but the only one in the house was at the end of the hall. She hesitated for a second and then opened her bedroom door and went out, feeling ridiculously like a naughty child.

It was like looking at a stranger, she thought in amazement as she gazed at her reflection—a complete stranger. Her hair was all wrong, of course, but it took just a minute to release it from its confines and brush it out so that it lay in thick curls on her shoulders.

With her hair down the transformation was complete. She looked younger, almost girlish—and pretty; she thought with surprise, I look pretty. She smiled at the thought and saw the stranger in the mirror smile back, only for the smile to be instantly wiped from her lips as another face appeared in the mirror behind her.

She whirled round just as Jack let out a slow, appreciative whistle. 'Excuse me,' she stammered, trying to sidestep him, her cheeks scarlet. 'I'm just going to change—'

'You mean there's a dress more stunning than that one? Now, this I've got to see,' he said, and smiled.

Never had she felt quite so exposed, so vulnerable. If only she hadn't tried on the wretched dress in the first place.

'You look lovely,' he said gently, sensing her embarrassment. 'I wouldn't change a thing—and I'm especially glad about your hair.'

'My hair?' she repeated, her hand going up to it instinctively.

'I've had a bet with myself ever since I first saw you

that you'd look great with it down and you do—oh, how you do.'

His compliment was genuinely meant—she knew it was—but she didn't know what to say. Fiona would have known. She would have said something light and frivolous that would have had Jack laughing, but she'd never been able to accept compliments; she'd always answered them in the past with a well-aimed snub.

'I really think I should put on something more suitable,' she muttered. 'I'm the local doctor—'

'And it's your day off,' he said firmly. 'And anyway there's no time,' he added, glancing at his watch. 'We'd better shoot off now if you don't want to be late—and I know how important punctuality is to you.'

She glanced up at him suspiciously. His face was totally bland but she was damn sure that there was laughter lurking at the back of his eyes. She'd pulled him up so many times about his own lack of punctuality—trust him to use that as a weapon against her.

'You're not going like that, are you?' she demanded, taking refuge in criticism as her eyes took in a pair of old denims cut above the knees and a vest-like T-shirt.

'I thought I'd go casual.'

'There's casual and there's totally laid back,' she protested, wondering how it was possible for any man to look so well in something so scruffy. 'You're the one representing the practice today, remember—when you judge the baby competition.'

'No one will bother about what I've got on my back,' he said dismissively.

Too damn right, she thought with irritation. He'd got everyone so happily eating out of his hand that he could probably have turned up in swimming trunks and no one would have batted an eyelid.

'My car or yours?' he asked, following her down the stairs.

She paused, deliberately averting her eyes from the pair of tanned, muscular legs behind her. 'When you say yours, do you mean the hire car or your old banger?'

'Depends on whether you actually want to get to this show or whether you'd like a day out with me in some cosy lay-by.' He grinned.

'We'll take the hire car,' she said firmly.

'Spoilsport!'

His eyes were brimming with laughter and she could not help but chuckle. 'You're an idiot, Jack Culrain!'

'My God, I'm actually going up in your estimation!' he exclaimed. 'Last week I was bloody arrogant, the week before I was a buffoon—what giddy heights will I reach by next week?'

'That of an even bigger fool?' she suggested, her eyes sparkling. 'Come on, we'd better get going.'

They did have difficulty in parking, as she had predicted. By the time they arrived at the large field outside the village, where Struan's Agricultural Show was held, there was scarcely a vacant parking space to be had.

''Struth—what a mob,' Jack declared in amazement as he gazed round at the mass of spectators.

'If you think this is busy you just wait until later. Oh, look—there's Fiona and her family,' she added, waving vigorously over the heads of those in front of her.

'Wowee—talk about someone hiding their light under a bushel,' Fiona exclaimed, dragging her husband and children towards them. 'You look sensational, Bridie!'

'Thanks.' She smiled. 'Any luck with your sheep this year, Robert?' she added, turning towards Fiona's husband—a solid, weather-beaten man with piercing blue eyes.

'A first for my ewe and a highly commended for the ram,' he replied.

'It was a fix,' Fiona declared stoutly. 'That judge wouldn't know a top-quality ram if it fell on him.'

'He'd sure as heck feel it, though.' Her husband grinned. 'I can't complain. George Hownam's ram was better on the day.'

Fiona's pursed lips showed that she for one didn't agree. 'Will you lot settle down, please?' she said as her two children tugged deliberately at her dress. 'Sorry about this, Jack, Bridie, but we were rash enough to promise them ice cream and they haven't shut up about it since. We'd better feed them, Robert—see you both later, I hope,' she added as she and her husband made their way to the ice-cream stall.

'The joys of parenthood,' Jack laughed.

'You've never been tempted yourself, then?' Bridie said curiously.

He gave a mock shudder. 'Heaven forbid!'

It was a pity, she thought. Having seen the way he'd handled Jamie Dunn when he'd had his asthma attack, she was sure that he'd make a good father.

'So, what do we do now?' he continued. 'Is there a received way of visiting this show or do you just dive in and hope to survive?'

'Most of the men hide in the beer tent all afternoon,' she observed.

'And you—what do you usually do?'

'I shop until my feet give out.' She chuckled.

'Mind if I tag along?'

'Feel free—but don't blame me if you get bored,' she said, leading the way into the throng.

As Fiona had said, there was a lot more to Struan Agricultural Show than just sheep and cattle. There were dozens of stalls—some selling a tempting array of cakes and candy, others selling beautifully made knitwear and lace, while still more sold exquisite hand-made crafts.

It was rumoured that you could buy anything at the Struan Show from a wedding dress to a carburettor, and after an hour of trying to keep up with Bridie Jack could well believe it.

'Don't you ever pause for breath?' he protested, staring pointedly at the many parcels under her arms.

'Sorry,' she said guiltily. 'Would you like some tea or coffee—or a beer, maybe?'

'You know what I'd really like to do?' he said, his eyes gleaming.

'What?' she asked warily.

'I'd like to try the amusements. I haven't done that since I was a kid.'

'Don't you men ever grow up?' she demanded. 'OK, OK, we'll go to the amusements,' she added as he managed to look quite ridiculously crestfallen. 'But I want no tears when you lose all your money!'

'O ye of little faith,' he declared, making a beeline for the shooting duck arcade.

'Fancy your chances, do you, Dr Culrain?' the stall-holder declared. 'All you have to do is hit six of the moving ducks and you can win a prize for your lovely girlfriend there.'

Bridie's cheeks pinkened, but Jack seemed unaware of it. He was too busy weighing the rifle thoughtfully in his hands.

'I'd be careful if I were you, Jack,' she warned, her lips twitching slightly. 'If you shoot yourself in the foot I haven't so much as a plaster with me!'

He threw her a look of lofty disdain, took careful aim, and to her amazement—and the clear dismay of the stallholder—he picked off six ducks, one after the other.

'Wherever did you learn to do that?' she exclaimed

as he pressed a lopsided toy rabbit triumphantly into her arms.

'Stick with me, kid,' he said smugly. 'You ain't seen nothing yet!'

And she hadn't. They hit the hoop-la, coconut shies and small pistol range in quick succession, and at each one he won a prize.

'Why do I have to have all these?' she demanded as he added the most hideous-looking doll she had ever seen to the rabbit, elephant and teddy bear that he had already won. 'You won them—you keep them.'

'What—hog all these wonderful prizes to myself?' He grinned.

She started to laugh. 'Oh, Jack, this is such—'

'Fun?'

She nodded.

'Good,' he said, smiling. 'That's exactly what I think you need—some fun.'

It had been years since she'd enjoyed herself so much. In fact, only one thing kept marring the day. No matter where she went she found herself being subjected to continual double takes as her patients walked straight past her, only to come running back a few moments later, offering profuse apologies, their eyes fixed on her with ill-disguised amazement.

'All this fuss because I've put on a dress,' she murmured uncomfortably. 'Anyone would think I'd grown two heads the way people are carrying on.'

'You can't expect people not to stare,' he replied. 'It must be quite a shock for them to discover they've been harbouring a butterfly all these years.'

She shook her head. 'Flattery will get you nowhere, Jack Culrain!'

He turned her round to him, his eyes searching her face. 'You really don't know, do you?' he said, with a puzzled frown. 'You really don't know you're beautiful.'

'I think I look pretty in this dress—'

'*Pretty*?' he exclaimed. 'That's like saying the Mona Lisa's not a bad painting.'

She laughed. 'You'd better watch it, Jack. One of these days I might actually start to believe some of what you say!'

'If I thought there was the remotest chance of that you'd hear a lot more, I can assure you,' he said softly.

A wave of colour crept over her cheeks at the look in his eyes and she gazed back at him pleadingly. 'Don't, Jack. Please. . .don't spoil it.'

He said nothing, his face unbelievably tender, and then he nodded. 'OK, sweetheart. Today we're just good friends—is that better?'

'Better.' She smiled tremulously.

'So what now?' he asked. 'The dodgems, the big wheel—?'

'Oh, damn!' she exclaimed as she glanced at her watch. 'It's time for the charity obstacle race, and Simon will never forgive me if I miss it.'

'And we can't possibly disappoint Simon, can we?' he said, his voice dry.

'It is for charity, Jack,' she protested.

'OK,' he sighed. 'Lead on.'

Fiona was already at the running track when they arrived. 'You look as though you've been having a good time,' she said approvingly, glancing from Bridie to Jack.

'We have.' Bridie smiled. 'I cleaned out the stalls and Jack bankrupted the amusements.'

'The perfect team, in other words,' Fiona declared, with a meaningful look that brought colour sweeping over Bridie's cheeks. 'There you are, Simon,' she added as he joined them. 'Where have you been hiding all afternoon—and, more to the point, what do you think of our new-look Dr McEwen?'

'Very nice, I'm sure,' he said, leaving Bridie with the distinct impression that for some reason he was not particularly pleased by her transformation.

'All ready for the big event, Simon?' Jack asked. 'Been doing some intensive training, have you?'

'I keep in good shape, if that's what you mean,' he replied tersely.

'I have to say it looks pretty taxing,' Jack continued, gazing out over the track.

'Let's just say it sorts out the men from the boys,' Simon observed, his lips curved into a disparaging smile.

'It's really only a bit of fun,' Bridie said quickly, seeing Jack's eyebrows snap down. 'No one takes it very seriously—'

'Simon does, don't you, Simon?' Fiona observed, clearly enjoying the situation hugely.

'If you mean that I always compete with the intention of winning, then, yes, I do take it seriously—very seriously.'

Jack's face set, but before he could reply they were joined by a distinctly grubby-looking Jamie Dunn.

'I've got my inhaler with me, Doctor, like you said I should,' he declared proudly, digging deep into his pocket and producing it.

'Well done.' Jack smiled, his face clearing.

'You're going to win the race, aren't you?' Jamie continued, his large brown eyes fixed admiringly on Jack. 'I told all my friends you would.'

'I'm afraid I'm a bit too long in the tooth for running, Jamie,' Jack declared apologetically.

The child's disappointment was clear. He scuffed his toes along the grass, his thin shoulders drooping. 'Mr Morrison's every bit as old as you are—older probably,' he said hopefully, 'and he didn't try out for Manchester United like you did. You'd walk it if only you'd enter; I know you would.'

A snort of smothered laughter came from Simon. 'Dr Culrain's hardly in peak physical condition, Jamie.'

'I'm damn sure I get more exercise than you do, Simon, cooped up in an operating room all day,' Jack said evenly, a faint flush of angry colour appearing on his cheeks.

Simon's eyebrows rose. 'Care to prove that by entering?'

'Now, hold on a minute,' Bridie said uncertainly. 'People have been known to get injured in this race, and a locum with a broken arm—Where the hell do you think you're going, Jack? Jack—you come back here right now!'

But it was too late; he had already gone.

Fiona's eyes sparkled with glee. 'This is going to be some race!'

'Some race? If he breaks an arm or a leg I'll kill him!' Bridie fumed.

'Who—Jack or Simon?'

'Jack, of course! How on earth does he think I'm going to run the practice if he gets injured?'

'You're sure that's all that's bothering you—the practice?' Fiona said quizzically.

'The whole thing's ridiculous,' Bridie declared, deliberately ignoring Fiona's question. 'The only reason he's taking part in this race is because he wouldn't back down in front of Jamie.'

Fiona shook her head. 'That's only part of it—he's competing for you.'

Bridie gazed at her for a moment, and then a peal of laughter broke from her. 'Oh, get real!'

'I'm serious,' Fiona replied. 'Jack and Simon are

jealous as hell of each other and they're in this race to try and impress you.'

'But that's—'

'Childish? Of course it is—but when were most men anything else?'

Bridie glanced pensively in the direction of the race-track. Fiona couldn't be right, surely, and, if she was, just how naïve could Jack and Simon get? As though it mattered a hill of beans to her which one of them won.

'They're off!' Fiona shouted as the sharp crack of the starter's gun split the air.

The noise was deafening. The vast majority of the competitors were either someone's dad, uncle, brother or husband—all in various states of unfitness, and all competing either for the fun of it or because they'd been press-ganged by members of their family. Family and friends whooped and yelled their encouragement, or subjected the entrants to catcalls of abuse.

Cheating was widespread as the competitors clambered up netting strung between two poles, vaulted over barrels and crawled through canvas tunnels, stopping at each obstacle to collect a different coloured balloon. The only serious competitors appeared to be Simon and Jack, and as they were roared on by the crowd Bridie found herself caught up in the excitement too.

Across the field she could see Liz Howard and her children jumping up and down, cheering Simon on, but her eyes followed only one man—a man in a pair of cut-off denims; a man with a shock of black hair—part of her cursing him for his stupidity and part of her willing him to win. And he did. To her complete surprise and delight he streaked through the tape just half a yard in front of Simon.

'Come on—let's congratulate him!' Fiona urged, dragging her across the field towards the finish line, where Jack was surrounded by cheering admirers.

'To the victor the spoils!' he declared, holding the tiny cup aloft and pushing his damp hair back from his forehead with clear delight. 'Would this triumph merit a kiss, Bridie?'

'A kiss?' she echoed, her face stern but her eyes betraying laughter. 'You just think yourself lucky you're still in one piece, Jack Culrain, because if you hadn't been I would have murdered you for leaving me short-handed!'

He sighed in mock resignation. 'I bring this woman the prize of the Struan Show and all I get is dog's abuse. What's a man got to do around here to get a little praise?'

'What he's told in future, I hope,' she said firmly. 'Oh, bad luck, Simon,' she added a little uncomfortably as he appeared at her side.

'The best man won on the day,' he said stiffly. 'I'm taking Liz Howard and her children for some afternoon tea—would you like to join us, Bridie?'

The invitation, she noticed, did not include Jack.

'I can't, I'm afraid,' she murmured. 'Jack's judging the baby competition in fifteen minutes and I really should give him moral support as it's his first time.'

'Suit yourself,' he said in clipped accents, and walked away.

She stared after him unhappily. Simon had been a good friend to her over the years, and the last thing she wanted was to hurt his feelings, but so much of her enjoyment of the day had been down to Jack and she was beginning to feel distinctly guilty about the competition.

'Hey, I don't need my hand held for this judging thing, you know,' Jack commented, following the direction of her gaze. 'Have tea with Simon—I'll catch up with you later.'

'Look, about the judging, Jack—'

'I told you before—it's a piece of cake.'

He strode purposefully away towards the marquee and a little voice urged her to call him back, to warn him about what he was letting himself in for, but an even louder demon whispered that it was time his overwhelming popularity took a dent. The demon won and she turned to Fiona quickly.

'Any chance of a lift home, Fiona? I'm feeling a bit tired—'

Fiona whooped with laughter. 'What you mean is you want to make a strategic retreat before all hell breaks loose! OK,' she continued, seeing Bridie's shamefaced grin, 'but I tell you this—I wouldn't like to be in your shoes when he gets back to the house!'

It was very nearly an hour and a half later before Bridie heard the front door slamming shut and the sound of Jack's feet taking the stairs two at a time.

He threw open the sitting-room door, his face stricken. 'You knew!' he said accusingly. 'You *knew*, and yet you let me walk into that lions' den unarmed! The only reason I'm still in one piece is because I made a run for it!'

'But just how hard can it be to judge the bonniest baby competition?' she reminded him, her eyes dancing. 'Anyone with half a brain can do it, can't they, Jack?'

'All right, all right,' he groaned. 'Don't gloat; it's not very appealing.'

'Maybe not, but it's sure as heck satisfying.' She chuckled. 'Who did you pick?'

'Mairi McDonald.'

She exploded. 'I'm surprised you made it from the field alive after that choice! She's the laird's daughter, Jack—everyone will think it was fixed.'

'I know that *now*,' he protested, 'but they were all such lovely babies I just chose one at random.'

'And you still managed to pick the wrong one,' she laughed. 'Oh, you idiot!'

'Don't rub it in,' he begged. 'You do realise I've only one choice now, don't you? I'll have to leave town.'

She shook her head. 'You'll be forgiven eventually, but your popularity's bound to have taken something of a nosedive. They take the bonniest baby competition very seriously round here.'

'You don't have to tell me that,' he said ruefully. 'I thought those mums and dads were going to lynch me.'

'I did try to warn you—'

'Like hell you did,' he said, advancing towards her, his eyes gleaming. 'You set me up, Bridie McEwen, and you're going to pay for it!'

A shriek of laughter came from her and she threw a cushion at him, but he avoided it neatly and pulled her to her feet, a broad grin on his face. 'Time for revenge, my dear!'

She didn't know quite when the laughter stopped. Perhaps it was when he slowly traced the outline of her cheek with his fingers; perhaps it was when she heard his breathing quicken as he drew her gently towards him. All she knew was that her heart began to race, and she put her hands against his chest quickly.

'No, Jack.'

'Don't you mean yes?' he murmured.

She shook her head, her eyes too large in her pale face. 'No, I mean no.'

'Why?' he demanded, his face puzzled.

'You and me—we're n-never going to be anything to each other—n-not now, not ever,' she stammered.

He cupped her face in his hands and felt her flinch. 'Bridie, sweetheart, tell me what's wrong.'

'It's been a long day,' she said, pulling herself free

and making for the door. 'I'm tired and I'm going to bed.'

She only just made her room in time. Tears trickled slowly down her cheeks as she pulled off her dress and threw it to the floor—tears of frustration and despair.

She was falling in love with him; she knew she was. He was all she'd ever wanted in a man—all she'd ever hoped for—but it was no use. No matter how she felt it was never going to be any use, and on that despairing thought she crept into bed and eventually fell asleep.

It had been years since she'd had the nightmare, but it was vivid as ever, as terrifying as ever. Always it began the same way, with Lucy's father smiling and teasing her, and then suddenly he wasn't smiling any more. Suddenly his face was ugly and twisted, and his hands were ripping at her clothes and body, and a monstrous obscenity was growing and growing between his legs.

And then the pain came—the excruciating pain—and she screamed and screamed as she always did for him to stop, but he wouldn't stop, and as she gasped and choked for breath the hands that held her tight became only stronger and tighter—

'Bridie—Bridie, wake up—it's Jack. Jack!'

She surfaced slowly, still fighting, still struggling against hands that were no longer imaginary but real, and found herself gazing up into a pair of brown eyes—eyes that were concerned, in a face that was gentle—and she broke down completely.

He cradled her in his arms, wiping her damp hair back from her forehead. Never had he heard anyone cry like this before—like an animal in pain. Great, racking sobs convulsed her whole body as she clung to him, tears spilling down her face, running into her nose and mouth as incoherent words tumbled out of her.

'Hush, hush, sweetheart. Oh, don't cry, Bridie, please don't cry,' he said huskily. 'Who are Lucy and Cameron—why are you so afraid of them?'

He was waiting for her to answer, and she knew she had to say something though her heart had grown cold. 'It. . .it was a dream, Jack, a nightmare—it means nothing.'

He swore gently under his breath. 'Why can't you trust me, Bridie? I know there's something wrong—something terribly wrong. Every time I try to touch you you push me away in panic. Whatever it is, whatever has happened to you, I promise I won't ever hurt you.'

The hard lump in her throat made speech impossible so she simply shook her head and tried to pull back, but he caught her hands in his.

'I mean it, my dear. You're safe with me. Can't you trust me, can't you tell me what's wrong?'

She fought against the tears that threatened to overwhelm her again. 'You don't. . .you don't understand, Jack.' Her voice was little more than a whisper.

'Try me. Tell me, Bridie.'

She wanted to tell him; she wanted him to understand that it wasn't him she was rejecting, but she was so ashamed. All the years of therapy she had undergone at the rape counselling centre had all been destroyed by Cameron, by the look in Cameron's eyes when she'd told him. And when he'd tried to make love to her—

'I don't want you to think. . .badly of me,' she faltered. 'I don't want you to be. . .disgusted.'

'Oh, Bridie, for God's sake, tell me what happened to you,' he said hoarsely. 'Whatever it is, nothing can be as bad as what I'm imagining.'

And so she told him. Slowly and haltingly she told him of Lucy's father—how kind he had been, how much fun, and how one day he had taken her on a picnic on her own.

'He said it was my fault,' she said, her lips trembling. 'He'd said if I told anyone about it my mother would go to prison. I believed him—for years I believed him. The first person I told was when I phoned the rape line at university.'

He held her tightly, rocking her in his arms, wishing he could blot out the memories for her, wishing none of it had ever happened as she told him about Cameron.

'He couldn't. . . I couldn't let him. . . I'm not. . .normal, Jack. I won't ever be. . .normal.'

Holding her away slightly, he lifted her head and forced her to look at him. 'You're a beautiful, wonderful, normal girl, Bridie,' he said fiercely. 'Some day you won't be frightened; some day you'll want someone and it will be all right.'

She shook her head in despair.

'You will!' he insisted. 'Maybe not next week, next month, but you will eventually—I promise.'

'And you're not—' Her voice broke. 'You're not. . .disgusted?'

He closed his arms around her again, tears pricking at the backs of his eyes. 'No, I'm not disgusted,' he said huskily. 'And now I think you should try and sleep. Will you be OK?'

She nodded, but her eyes told him otherwise.

'Look, I'll sleep with you tonight—'

With a smothered cry she backed away from him, and he caught her shoulders quickly.

'I said *sleep* with you, Bridie, not make love to you. I'll hold you for comfort's sake and I'll be there if you need me. I'm not asking for anything more, I promise.'

She gazed at him searchingly for a long moment and

then slowly moved over to the far side of the bed. He slipped in beside her, easing his arm gently under her shoulders, and then lay completely motionless, though he was all too aware of her nearness.

At first she lay totally rigid next to him, her breath coming in ragged gasps, but gradually he felt her relax, and at last she turned tentatively towards him and curled up against his side. Deliberately he didn't turn his head, sensing the courage it had taken her to get that far, and eventually, with a small sigh, she laid her head on his chest and fell asleep.

Sleep did not come easily to him. For a long time he lay staring at the ceiling, watching the shadows as the moon travelled across the sky. In all his life he had never felt such compassion for another human being, and in all his life he had never felt such anger and such hatred as he felt towards the two men who had so hurt her.

CHAPTER SIX

It was the insistent warble of birdsong outside her window that woke Bridie the next morning with a start. She yawned and stretched, and then she remembered. For a moment she didn't move, and then slowly, hesitantly she turned. There was no one in the bed beside her. The place where Jack had slept was still warm but he wasn't there.

She closed her eyes tightly and rolled onto her side, hugging her knees to her chest. It was only half past six, scarcely dawn, but she couldn't blame Jack for leaving her so soon. Cameron had been the same. He'd wanted to get away from her as quickly as he could.

The sound of her bedroom door opening had her sitting bolt-upright immediately, clutching the bedcover to her throat.

'Did I wake you?' Jack apologised, standing hesitantly in the doorway. 'I tried to be as quiet as I could but I was desperate for a cup of coffee.'

She said nothing, wishing she was anywhere but here. The man who stood before her wearing only his pyjama trousers seemed to fill the room with his masculine presence. Last night she had been scarcely aware of it. Last night she had thought of him only as a shadowy, comforting figure in the dark—a rock she could cling to—and now. . .

'Would you like it? The coffee, I mean,' he continued, holding the mug out to her. 'I can easily get myself another.'

She took the mug from his outstretched hand and gulped the contents down quickly, though it scalded her throat and tongue. To her strained nerves his voice sounded distant, awkward. He was clearly just as uncomfortable with the situation as she was, she thought wretchedly.

'Bridie—'

'You don't have to say anything,' she said quickly. 'I know how. . .how embarrassing this must be for you. I shouldn't have told you what I did; I wouldn't have if I'd not—' She bit her lip savagely. 'If you want to leave right away, rather than working out the next six weeks, I'll quite understand.'

She couldn't believe how calm she sounded, how poised, and he clearly couldn't believe it either, for he sat down on the edge of her bed, his face puzzled.

'Leave?' he echoed. 'Why on earth would you think I wanted to leave?' Unconsciously her eyes drifted to the empty space in the bed between them, and understanding appeared on his face. 'You thought I'd shot out of bed because of what you told me—that's it, isn't it?'

'Isn't it?' she murmured, pleating and unpleating her fingers in her lap.

He shook his head, his eyes tender. 'I told you that I was a caffeine addict and I am. I got up to get a coffee and a pair of socks.'

'Socks?' she repeated, bewildered.

His lips curved into a smile. 'Your bed's too damn short, my dear. I woke up thinking I had frostbite.'

An answering smile appeared on her face for an instant and then was gone. 'You do know it's going to be impossible for us to work together now, don't you?'

'Why?' he exclaimed. 'Oh, sweetheart, what do you think I'm going to do—drag up your past every five minutes, dissect it, examine it, or jump on you and try and effect a "cure"?'

She stirred uneasily in the bed and he took the empty mug from her gently.

'I won't deny that I want you, Bridie, but I'm not going to pressurise you—not in any shape or form. You call the tune from now on; you set the pace. And now I really must get myself that coffee,' he added, getting to his feet with a grin. 'I'm gasping.'

'Jack.'

He paused.

'Don't. . .don't expect anything from me,' she said slowly. 'Don't hope for too much.'

'Hey, did no one ever tell you I'm the eternal optimist?' He smiled. 'Scrambled eggs and bacon for breakfast suit?'

'You're cooking for me?' she said in surprise.

'Why not? It's just as easy to make for two as it is for one.'

'Jack.' He was already halfway to the door but he turned questioningly. She took a deep breath. 'I just wanted to say. . .thank you.'

'I told you I was a New Age man,' he said, bowing with an extravagant flourish.

'I don't mean for breakfast—'

'I know you don't,' he said, his expression kind, and then his eyes began to dance, 'because if you'd ever tasted my cooking you sure as heck wouldn't be thanking me, I can assure you!'

She began to laugh, all tension gone from her.

'That's better,' he declared approvingly. 'It's a new day, Bridie, and it can be a new beginning if you'll let it. The past can't be erased but you have to go forward some time, and today is as good a day as any to start. Breakfast in half an hour if that's OK?'

She nodded and he was gone.

She got up, feeling as though a heavy weight had suddenly been lifted from her shoulders. He knew everything about her past and he didn't care; he knew what had happened and yet he hadn't turned from her in horror.

Perhaps he was right; perhaps it was time to start moving on—time to leave the past behind. She'd been so dominated by her memories for all these years that she'd never looked forward. All she'd ever thought was that her future would be a continuation of her past. Now he was telling her that it didn't have to be like that, and she was starting to believe him.

Quickly she threw open her wardrobe door. The hot weather had broken overnight and heavy, thundery rain was bouncing off the roof and lying in puddles in the street. She couldn't wear the dress she'd had on yesterday and the only other dress she possessed would be just as impracticable. With a sigh she took out her sensible navy suit and put it on.

Her chestnut hair was a tangled mass of curls after her restless night and she brushed it through vigorously and then began twisting it up into its customary chignon, only to stop as she caught a glimpse of her reflection in the dressing-table mirror. She stared at herself for a moment and then pulled out all the hairpins again and let her hair fall around her shoulders. It was a new day, a new start, as Jack had said.

'Bacon's done and eggs are just about ready,' he declared as she came into the kitchen. His eyes travelled over her. 'Hair's fine—shame about the suit.'

'So Fiona told me yesterday,' she said drily, taking a seat at the kitchen table and making a mental note to visit a dress shop as soon as she could.

'I'd better eat mine quickly,' he said as he put a steaming plate of bacon and eggs in front of her, 'or I'll end up infringing on your half-hour in the kitchen.'

Deliberately she stretched behind her and, taking

the kitchen rota down from the cupboard door, tore it in two.

His eyes lit up. 'Hallelujah! If there's one thing I hate it's eating on my own. Hey, I don't suppose you would consider—?' He came to a halt.

'You don't suppose I would consider what?' she asked, her mouth full of eggs.

'You wouldn't consider cooking for us both from now on, would you?' Her eyebrows rose and he rushed on quickly. 'I'm a lousy cook, Bridie—bacon and eggs are about the only thing I don't ruin—and—'

'And as I'm a woman I should be the one in the kitchen,' she finished for him. 'Forget it, Jack. My schedule's just as busy as yours is.' His face fell quite ludicrously, and despite herself she began to laugh. 'OK, OK, I'm a sucker for a sob story—always have been—but I'm not going to do all the cooking. You've got to do your fair share—understood?'

'Understood.' He nodded vigorously and she smiled wryly. Why did she have the feeling that the most she could expect from him when it was his turn in the kitchen was bacon and eggs or a plate of sandwiches?

'Is it safe to come in?' a familiar voice called warily from outside the kitchen door.

'Of course it is, Fiona,' Bridie laughed.

'Why wouldn't it be safe?' Jack questioned curiously as Fiona helped herself to a cup of coffee and then joined them at the table. 'And, more to the point, what are you doing here at quarter past seven on a Monday morning?'

'I thought I'd better come in early in case there was any cleaning up to do,' Fiona declared, her brown eyes sparkling. 'Blood stains on the floor, Bridie requiring a piece of steak for her eye—that sort of thing.'

'I presume you're suggesting Bridie and I might have come to blows over the bonniest baby competition?'

Jack said loftily, but with a deliberate wink at Bridie. 'I'm sorry to disappoint you, Fiona, but we are civilised, professional people.'

'In other words, Bridie was too quick on her feet for you!' Fiona chuckled. She said no more until Jack had gone off to shower and then she turned to Bridie eagerly. 'OK—confession time. What really happened when he got back to the house last night?' Unconsciously Bridie's face softened and Fiona's face broke into a broad smile. 'You told him, didn't you—about what happened to you—and he didn't give a damn, did he?'

Bridie shook her head.

'Oh, he's so right for you,' Fiona said triumphantly. 'I knew it the first minute I laid eyes on him. He's a doctor like you, so you've lots in common, and he's handsome enough to die for—'

'Hey, hold onto your horses a minute!' Bridie protested. 'All that happened was I told him—'

'Yes, but who knows what the future might bring—?'

'At the moment one nice, long shower for me, and this to keep you from talking rubbish,' Bridie said, popping a piece of toast into Fiona's open mouth and then making good her escape, laughing as she heard her receptionist's spluttered protests.

It was a long morning. The Donaldson triplets came in for the start of their immunisation programme, and it only took one of them to start crying before the others joined in at the top of their lungs. Mrs Gourlay went off in a huff when Bridie refused to give her any more sleeping pills, and Alec Murray—big, six feet four, strapping Alec Murray—point-blank refused to let her give him a tetanus injection.

'There's no need, Doc,' he said, edging towards the door. 'It was just a little accident—the garden fork slipping like that and going into my foot—and you've cleaned the wound up a treat—that'll do me fine.'

'Don't tell me you're afraid of a little needle, Alec?' she said in her best wheedling tone.

'Certainly not,' he said stoutly, his barrel-like chest expanding indignantly at the very thought. 'The original macho man—that's me. I just don't see the point in having something unnecessary, that's all.'

'You prefer to have lockjaw then?'

He blanched. 'Lockjaw?'

'Anyone who lives in the country or does a lot of gardening is leaving themselves wide open to lockjaw if they don't have a tetanus injection after an accident,' she declared.

'Ideally, everyone who works in any way with the soil should have a course of tetanus injections as a routine precaution rather than waiting until they've had an accident. The tetanus bacteria is widespread in the soil, you see, and all it takes is a little scratch from something as simple as a thorn for it to get into the body.'

Alec had gone quite green. 'What. . .what happens then?' he asked weakly.

'Well, the first symptoms are stiffness in the jaw and spine, and after that the jaw locks and the muscular spasms begin. You know,' she added reminiscently, 'I've seen cases of muscular spasm that were so bad the patient actually fractured parts of his back—it was fascinating to watch, absolutely fascinating. And, of course, without hospital treatment,' she continued relentlessly, 'tetanus is usually fatal.'

There was a loud clatter as Alec hit the floor in a dead faint, and she lifted the syringe with a sigh. 'OK, Mr Macho Man,' she announced as she advanced purposefully towards him, 'one injection coming up.'

'Good grief, what happened?' Jack asked as he came

in at a run to see her bending over Alec Murray's bare backside. 'Fiona heard the thud and came for me—'

'Panic over,' she replied. 'All you see here is a fine example of male ego biting the dust. Alec decided he didn't want a tetanus injection,' she explained as he eyed her quizzically, 'so I decided to explain to him—in somewhat graphic terms—why he should have one.'

'Then all I can say is I hope you don't ever have to give me any bad news if this is an example of your bedside manner,' he laughed.

She chuckled. 'He'll be OK in a few minutes, apart from a very sore backside. Are there any more patients out there?'

He frowned. 'Just one.'

'From the expression on your face I take it Mrs Findlay's back from Inverness?' she sighed.

He shook his head. 'It's Elsa Livingstone. Ostensibly she's come to have the dressing on her arm changed again, but she's sporting one very obvious black eye.'

She swore softly. 'I hate to say it, Jack, but I have a dreadful feeling you might be right about her.'

'Would you like me to sit in on this one with you?' he asked.

'No—thanks for the offer—but no. I've known Elsa a lot longer than you have and I think I might get more out of her on my own.'

'OK, but I'll be upstairs if you need me.'

As Jack had said, Elsa Livingstone's black eye was a spectacular one, but Bridie deliberately ignored it and concentrated on changing the dressing on her arm before she mentioned it.

'Oh, it was the stupidest thing to do, Doctor,' Elsa declared, trying to smile and not succeeding. 'I was cleaning the kitchen floor and forgot I'd left one of the unit doors open. When I stood up, this was the result.'

'Are you sure that's how it happened?' Bridie said gently.

Elsa stared down at her work-worn hands, her faded grey eyes suddenly brimming with unshed tears. 'I'm just getting old, Doctor—careless, you know. It happens to us all eventually.'

Bridie made up her mind quickly. 'I'm not happy about all these accidents you keep having, Elsa, and I'd like to examine you. It's probably nothing serious,' she added as Elsa made to interrupt. 'It could simply be that you have an inner ear problem that's affecting your balance, but I do want to examine you—so if you could just slip behind the screens and undress for me—'

Elsa Livingstone was on her feet immediately. 'I really don't have the time today, Doctor. My neighbour brought me down to the surgery, you see, and I don't like to keep her waiting when she's been so kind.'

'I'm sure she won't mind waiting just a few minutes,' Bridie said smoothly. 'The examination won't take very long and I really do think it would be for the best.'

'But, Doctor—'

'Ten minutes of your time, Elsa, that's all it will take, but if it's difficult today I could always come over to your home and carry out the examination there?'

The suggestion hung in the air between them and Bridie saw panic and indecision warring with one another in the old lady's eyes and then her shoulders slumped.

'All right, Doctor, if you insist,' she muttered in defeat, and went behind the screens.

While she waited for Elsa to undress Bridie looked through her file. Nothing in it suggested that Elsa was suffering from Alzheimers—that devastating disease that robbed the mind of memory and recognition—but though she had little time for Bill Livingstone as a man she couldn't believe he would actually hit his mother.

She'd read about it happening, of course—cases of granny-bashing, they called it down south—but surely it wasn't possible that it could happen here, in Struan, and no one would know about it?

Andrew used to joke that it was impossible for anyone to sneeze in the community without the whole neighbourhood talking about it the next day, and she had never heard so much as a whisper, far less a rumour.

She got to her feet and went round the screens, and only just crushed down the involuntary gasp that sprang to her lips. Elsa Livingstone's frail body was a mass of bruises. Some of them were old, some more recent, but by no stretch of the imagination could they all have been acquired accidentally.

Seeing the direction of her gaze, Elsa flushed deeply. 'As you can see, I'm a bit accident-prone, Doctor.'

'Oh, Elsa, no one's that accident-prone. Someone's hit you. Who did this to you? Was it. . .was it Bill?'

Tears welled in Mrs Livingstone's eyes and she rubbed them away vigorously. 'I make him angry sometimes—when I'm late with his dinner. It's my fault—'

'How can it be your fault?' Bridie demanded, fighting to control the overwhelming anger she felt. 'How can you have done anything that warrants you being treated like this?'

Mrs Livingstone smiled tremulously. 'He's a good boy at heart. I do silly things—'

'No one has the right to hit you, Elsa—no one!' Bridie cried. 'Does Alice know about this—have you told your daughter?'

Panic appeared in Mrs Livingstone's eyes. 'You mustn't tell her, Doctor. I don't want her upset. She's a good job down in Edinburgh and I don't want—'

'But what Bill is doing to you is a criminal offence,' Bridie declared, taking Elsa's hands in hers. 'The police—'

'I'm not calling the police!' Elsa exclaimed vehemently. 'He's my son and sometimes he has too much to drink and then he gets angry—that's all it is.'

Bridie bit her lip with frustration. 'Elsa, what if he really hurts you one day? What if he does you some serious damage?'

'He won't; I know he won't,' Elsa said firmly. 'He loves me—I'm his mother. He would never hurt his own mother.'

Bridie argued and cajoled but nothing she said would persuade Mrs Livingstone to go to the police, and eventually she had to let her go.

Slowly she went up to the kitchen, anger seething through her.

'I can see by your face that I was right,' Jack sighed as he handed her a cup of coffee. 'Her son's hitting her?'

'She believes he doesn't mean it, that it's all her own fault,' Bridie cried. 'How can such a dear, sweet old lady be at fault? My God, even if she was a huge, strapping woman no man has a right to hit her. It makes me so mad—'

'I take it she won't prosecute?'

'Not a hope in hell.'

'Well, if she won't prosecute I'm afraid there's nothing we can do.'

'So we just have to wait, do we?' she demanded furiously. 'Do nothing until she's hospitalised or worse? A fat lot of use you are!'

'Hey—I'm on your side, remember?' he said gently.

His deep brown eyes showed such sympathy and understanding that she stretched out her hand to him and he held it tight. 'I'm sorry, Jack—I shouldn't be taking it out on you, but it's so—'

'Frustrating?' He nodded. 'It always is in a situation like this, but you know our position as well as I do. Unless the patient goes to the police themselves we can't interfere. All you can do is try and make her change her mind. Would you like me to have a word?'

'Would you?' she said eagerly. 'Use the famous Culrain charm—use any weapon you can—but get her to see sense, Jack. I'm so afraid that if this goes on there will come a time when I'm not treating her for another injury but signing her death certificate.'

'If she won't listen to reason I could always arrange to "accidentally" reverse my car over her son,' he mused thoughtfully.

'If it comes down to that I'll do it myself with pleasure,' she said deliberately.

'Good idea. With your standard of driving it shouldn't occasion much comment.'

'Wretch!' she laughed, aiming a mock punch at him. 'That's not what I meant at all, and you know it!'

He grinned, pleased to see her face relaxing into less rigid lines. 'I'll give it my best shot, Bridie, but I can't promise anything. The only person who can do anything in this situation is Mrs Livingstone herself. And now I'd better get on before my morning calls think I've got lost.'

She nodded and accompanied him downstairs.

'I hope you're going to put your feet up for the rest of the day,' he continued as they reached the front door. 'You didn't get much sleep last night and you look tired—'

'Thanks a million!'

The corners of his mouth curved slightly. 'You know very well what I mean, so don't fish for compliments.'

She chuckled. 'I wasn't, I can assure you.'

'I know.' He smiled. 'You're the least vain woman

I've ever met. So, are you going to take the doctor's advice and relax?'

'I will after I've taken a quick drive across to the hospital. It's Kirsty Ferguson, Jack,' she added quickly as his black eyebrows snapped down. 'She's been in a coma now for four days, and her parents are devastated. When we resuscitated her—after she was hit by that car—I wondered, with her head wound and with her not breathing for so long—'

'When are you going to learn that you can't take all the cares and woes of the world onto your shoulders?' he interrupted vexedly.

'I don't!' she exclaimed. 'Kirsty's a bit special, that's all. She was the very first patient I treated when I came here five years ago, so it's only natural I'll have a soft spot for her.'

'It's not just Kirsty; you know it's not,' he declared. 'You agonise over each and every one of your patients, little one.'

'I don't,' she insisted, only to see his eyebrows rise quizzically. 'OK, maybe I do,' she continued reluctantly, 'but I'm not little,' she added inconsequentially. 'I'll have you know I'm five feet eight in my stockinged soles.'

He touched the top of her head gravely, but with laughter in his brown eyes, and then measured it against his broad chest. 'You are little to me, little one.'

The touch of his hand was fleeting, but that and his words seemed to wrap around her heart, comforting and warming it.

'I won't stay long with Kirsty, I promise,' she said.

'See you don't.'

'I hope you're not going to get all bossy on me, are you?' she protested.

'Someone has to,' he said as he got into his car. 'And I've decided it might as well be me.'

He drove away, leaving her standing gazing after him. To have someone concerned about her, to have someone want to take care of her was a new experience, and she discovered she liked it—she liked it very much.

Cameron hadn't wanted to take care of her. He had wanted to possess her, in the way a collector wanted to possess a beautiful, perfect ornament, and when he'd discovered that she wasn't perfect but flawed, and flawed in a way he couldn't repair, he'd walked away.

From that day on she had retreated into her shell, hiding behind her unflattering clothes and hairstyle, keeping the world at arm's length with a sharp tongue and abrasive manner.

She had told herself that she could be happy as an independent career woman, that her work could fulfil her as much as any relationship could, but she knew now that it couldn't. She wanted more—much more—and all she needed now was to find the courage to take it.

She drove to the hospital more slowly than usual, part of her remembering Jack's jibe about her driving, the other part reluctant to face what she might find when she got there.

As she had feared, there was no change in Kirsty's condition. She was still in Intensive Care, her breathing and fluid intake measured and controlled by a battery of sophisticated machines.

A team of dedicated doctors and nurses were monitoring her round the clock, but an air of resignation was beginning to creep into the ward. Only Kirsty's parents clung on, white-faced, to the hope that she would recover, but even they were now clinging to that hope with quiet desperation—a desperation Bridie could not find the words to ease.

She left the ward despondently, all too conscious of

how inadequate medical science was in the face of such odds, and almost collided with Simon Morrison.

'You look as though you've got all the cares and woes of the world on your shoulders,' he said, smiling.

She returned his smile with an effort. 'I've just been in to see Kirsty Ferguson.'

'It's not good, as you'll have seen,' he replied. 'We're checking for signs of brain activity, and if there's none. . .'

She nodded. If Kirsty was pronounced brain dead there would be no way back for her. 'Where are you off to in such a rush?' she asked, forcing her thoughts to the back of her mind.

'I'm taking Liz and her kids sailing.'

'Liz? You mean Liz Howard from Men's Surgical?'

He nodded, a faint flush of colour in his cheeks. 'The kids told me yesterday they'd never been out on a boat so I've offered to take them.'

'That's really nice of you, Simon,' she said genuinely. 'Liz will enjoy it, I'm sure.'

'You don't mind?' he said, his eyes fixed on her face. 'Me taking Liz and her kids out?'

'Why on earth should I?' she asked.

'That's the trouble, isn't it, Bridie?' he said, with a sad smile. 'You really don't mind, do you?'

She gazed at him awkwardly. 'Simon, I've always been straight with you. I've always told you that we'd never be anything but good friends.'

'I know, but I kept on hoping—'

'Then stop,' she said gently. 'I'm sorry if I'm hurting you—truly I am—but I can't change the way I feel. Now I'd better go,' she added quickly. 'I promised Jack this would be a short visit, and if he finds out just how long I've been here I'll get my head in my hands.'

She walked along the corridor, only to discover that he had followed her.

'Arc you sure you know what you're doing, Bridie?'

She stopped. 'What do you mean?'

'You and Jack.'

She laughed a little shakily. 'There is no me and Jack, Simon. He's a friend—just as you are.'

'I don't remember you ever changing your clothes and hairstyle for me,' he replied pointedly.

'A girl's got a right to change her image once in a while, hasn't she?' she said, fighting to restrain her mounting colour.

He sighed. 'I. . .care about you, Bridie, and I don't want to see you hurt. Jack's a locum—one of the here-today-and-gone-tomorrow brigade.'

'Andrew's hoping he'll stay on,' she said defensively. 'He's thinking of retiring, and he's hoping to persuade Jack to come into the practice.'

'And you—what are you hoping?' he asked, his face pensive.

'Jack's a good doctor; he gets on well with the patients; he's beginning to know the area—'

'You're a rotten liar, Bridie,' he said wryly. 'If Jack's the one you want then so be it and good luck to you, but can you really see him staying on here? Do you really think this little part of Scotland is big enough for him?'

'It's up to Jack to decide what he wants,' she said firmly, 'and anyway nothing's definite at the moment. Andrew might change his mind, and then there would be no vacancy.'

Simon shook his head. 'If Andrew's even suggested retiring then it's as good as definite. I hope it works out for you, Bridie, I really do. There's no one who deserves to be happy more than you do, but are you sure Jack's the right man? Only a short while ago you told me he was impossible to work with, that he was arrogant and opinionated.'

'Simon—'

'And what do you really know about him, about his past?' he persisted. 'All you know is that he never stays very long in one place, which doesn't suggest he's exactly the most reliable of men. I don't want you to make a fool of yourself, my dear.'

Hot anger flashed in her heather-coloured eyes. 'There are times when even good friends overstep the mark, Simon, and this is one of them. Thanks for your concern but I'm a big girl; I know what I'm doing.'

It was only when she reached her car that she allowed herself to think about what he'd said.

Simon was right. There had been a time when the one thing she'd wanted most in the world was to see the back of Jack Culrain, but now she couldn't even begin to imagine what her life would be like without him. Slowly and insidiously he had somehow managed to charm his way round her defences, and yet what did she really know about him other than what he had told her?

It doesn't matter, she told herself firmly; it isn't important. The only important thing is that he's here.

Yes, but for how long? a small voice whispered as she got into the car. He'd only come to Struan to fill in his time before he went to a new post in the States, and he only agreed to stay on longer because Andrew had been injured.

But things are different now, aren't they? she told herself uncertainly. Andrew was talking of retiring and Jack liked the area, she was sure he did, and he fitted in well in the community. Oh, get real, Bridie, the small voice said mockingly. Which would you choose if you were an ambitious doctor like Jack—a rural backwater like Struan or the land of opportunity, the States?

'You're not just looking for bridges to cross, Bridie

McEwen, you're building them too,' she muttered out loud. 'Accept and enjoy what you have here and now.'

And with that she drove away from the hospital, resolutely pushing the small, warning voice to the back of her mind.

CHAPTER SEVEN

THE news from the hospital about Kirsty Ferguson's condition grew ever more discouraging as the next couple of days progressed. Bridie did what she could to help ease the anguish of the girl's parents but it was exhausting both mentally and physically, trying to juggle her time between their needs and the needs of the practice.

Old Mr Brownlie, who had been so critical of her when she first arrived in Struan, had a heart attack late Tuesday night and died on his way to hospital, one of the Donaldson triplets took a flying leap off a seat and broke an arm, and, just when Bridie thought she'd had enough, late on Wednesday afternoon Fiona brought the glad tidings that Mrs Findlay was back from her visit to her daughter in Inverness.

'Don't tell me she wants an appointment already?' she groaned.

Fiona nodded. 'Tomorrow, if possible, she said—quite frankly I don't see how she can have had time to unpack, far less go down with anything, but there it is.'

'If it's that urgent you'd better book her in for half past nine tomorrow, then.'

'But Jack's taking surgery tomorrow,' Fiona declared.

'I know,' Bridie said mischievously, and Fiona shook her head and chuckled. 'Is there something else?' she continued as her receptionist hovered uncertainly at the door.

'No—nothing,' Fiona began, and then quickly took a seat, her eyes sparkling. 'Oh, all right, I'll confess.

I just can't stand this suspense. You and Jack—any developments?'

Bridie gave her a hard stare. 'Anyone ever tell you you're nosy?'

'Frequently. So put me out of my misery and tell me what's new.'

'Nothing.'

Fiona pouted. 'You're a gossip's nightmare, do you know that, Bridie McEwen?'

'I'm very glad to hear it.' Bridie grinned.

'And are you just as glad to hear that Simon has been seeing a lot of Liz Howard lately?'

'Where on earth do you get your information from?' Bridie exclaimed, half laughing. 'Well, for once I hope the grapevine's right. They're well suited.'

'Like you and Jack.'

Bridie shook her head. 'Stop stirring, Fiona.'

'You can't blame a girl for trying,' Fiona protested. 'There's nothing I'd like better than to see you with someone in your life, though I have to say that in Jack's current mood he's not exactly Prince Charming, is he?'

'I don't know what's eating him,' Bridie admitted, with a frown. 'Normally he's so easy-going, but these last few days he's been going about like a bear with a sore head.'

'You don't have to tell me,' Fiona replied, and then lapsed into embarrassed silence as Jack suddenly appeared at the kitchen door.

'There's a stack of referrals needing your attention in the office, Fiona,' he said sharply.

'I was just going—'

'Then don't let me keep you.'

Fiona made herself scarce, with a backward glance of resignation at Bridie.

'That wasn't necessary, Jack,' Bridie commented as she poured him out a cup of coffee. 'Fiona's a hard worker. She might be a bit chatty, but I'd rather she was like that—'

'What time did you get to bed last night?' he interrupted tightly.

'What?' she said, confused by the unexpected turn of the conversation.

'I said, what time did you get to bed last night?'

'Around one, I think.'

'Liar. I heard you creeping in at three.'

'Then why ask me if you know already?' she returned evenly.

'Because I'm worried about you, goddamn it,' he declared. 'Can't you see that you're running yourself into the ground? It's hard enough just to cope with surgeries, morning rounds and the odd emergency, without you spending all your free time at the hospital with the Fergusons. I insist you stop this.'

She put down his cup with a bang, sending tiny droplets of coffee showering over the table.

'Oh, you *insist* do you? Now listen here, Jack Culrain, the day my patients start suffering from any action of mine is the day you can interfere in my professional life, and not before. I'm not neglecting my duties; I've not asked you to do any of my shifts—good God, I even do the cooking when it's my turn—'

'And when do you ever eat any of it?' he demanded, his colour high. 'All I ever see you with is a sandwich in your hand as you go out the door.'

'I am not a little girl so don't treat me like one,' she said coldly, though her eyes flashed fire. 'I don't need a minder to tell me how much sleep I should get, what meals I should eat, so back off, Jack!'

'So you're just going to go on like this, are you?' he said furiously. 'Driving yourself too hard until you end up in hospital with nervous exhaustion?'

She took a step towards him quickly, her face white

with anger, and then suddenly stopped. 'What the hell are we doing here, Jack?' she murmured, bewildered. 'We're halfway towards having a full-scale row and I don't even know why.'

The fury died in his face and he shook his head ruefully. 'I'm angry because I'm worried about you, little one.'

She bit her lip. 'I know you mean well but I have to go to the hospital. Kirsty's parents are in such a state—'

'And the hospital's full of doctors and nurses who can comfort them.'

'Kirsty's just another patient to them—I've known her and her family since I came here. Look, I know you told me once that you make it a golden rule never to get involved with your patients, but I can't work like that, Jack, I just can't.'

'Bridie—'

'And I don't think you can either,' she continued firmly. 'You wouldn't have stayed up half the night last week with old Mrs Ogilvie if you didn't care—you would just have told her husband to get on with it.'

He smiled ruefully. 'OK, so you've rumbled me, but I'm worried about you.'

'And I appreciate your concern,' she said softly, gazing up into his deep brown eyes, 'but I have to do this. I have this dreadful feeling, you see, that the end isn't very far away.'

He sighed. 'You just won't be looked after, will you?'

'I will if I need it, but on this occasion I don't, honestly.' She smiled. 'And, anyway, since when did you go into the adoption business?'

She was right, he thought with a sudden shock. Adopting waifs and strays wasn't his style at all. Indeed, if someone had told him that in the space of a few short weeks he would have spent so much of his time not just wanting a woman but worrying about her, he would have told them that they needed their head examined.

And he did worry about her. He worried about whether she was getting enough to eat, he worried about if she was getting enough rest and he worried in case she was doing too much. Hell and damnation, he thought angrily, he couldn't have watched her more closely if she'd been a sister he was concerned about. But she wasn't his sister, and the feelings he had for her were not those a brother would have felt.

A brother would not have been so intensely aware of the slender thighs beneath her new pencil-slim skirts; a brother would not have been so acutely conscious of the swell of her breasts under her fashionable silk blouses. When she looked up and laughed with genuine amusement at something he'd said it took all of his resolve not to take her in his arms. When she unconsciously brushed against him when they were discussing case notes her closeness drove him crazy.

Day by day he knew that she was growing more and more comfortable in his presence while he was growing less and less at ease in hers, and he was finding it harder and harder to keep his promise that she could set the pace.

'Is there anybody in there?'

'Sorry?' he said in confusion.

She laughed. 'I just asked you whether there were any problems with this morning's surgery and I could have sworn you said "so much for a sister".'

A faint tinge of colour crept across his cheeks. 'Surgery was pretty uneventful. John Harvey and his wife came in. I don't know who looks worse—Mrs Harvey or her husband.'

'She's so worried about him, and I can't say I blame

her,' Bridie observed. 'Did none of the checks on the rest of the family show anything?'

'Not a thing. They're all fit as fiddles. I'm going to ring the lab this afternoon and see if I can't get them to hurry up his blood samples a bit—they might be able to tell us something.'

She sighed. 'It's so ironic—John moved to the country for a healthier lifestyle and now he's just fading away—'

'He's not local, then?' Jack interrupted.

'He was an insurance agent in Inverness, but he was made redundant three years ago and decided to use his redundancy money to buy the dairy farm.'

'A dairy farm,' he repeated, his eyebrows knitting slightly.

'I know it seems a bit of a quantum leap from being in insurance, but it isn't really. His father used to breed sheep in Argyllshire. . .' She came to a halt, aware that he wasn't listening to her. 'What are you thinking?'

'I've had an idea—it might be something, it might be nothing,' he murmured, and then smiled as he saw her gazing speculatively at him. 'Let me run it past the boffins in the blood lab first—it could be just another blind alley.'

She nodded, waited for a moment as he sipped his coffee and then gave in. 'Do I have to drag it out of you or are you going to tell me?'

'Tell you what?'

'Elsa Livingstone. You said you were going to call on her yesterday, and you haven't told me how you got on.'

'Perhaps if I actually got the chance to talk to you once in a while, instead of just seeing your back as you shoot out the door—'

'OK, OK, we've covered that ground already,' she

said wryly. 'Elsa—did you have any luck?'

He shook his head. 'She made me a cup of tea, politely listened to all I had to say, and then just as politely told me to mind my own business. I'll keep on trying, but short of forcibly removing her from her cottage there's nothing else I can do.'

Bridie frowned, and then a small smile appeared on her lips. 'There's nothing else *we* can do, no, but there's someone who might be able to make her listen to reason.'

Jack's brows lowered. 'Whatever plan is revolving round that fertile little brain of yours, drop it. Consultations are supposed to be as private as the confessional box, and if you bring in a third party you could be in deep trouble if the BMA find out.'

'I know.'

'So you'll drop it—whatever it is you're thinking of doing?' She stared down into her coffee. 'Bridie—'

'The phone's ringing.' She smiled sweetly.

He lifted it, scowling at her belligerently, and then his expression changed. His answers to whoever was on the other end of the line were abrupt, terse.

'What's up?' she asked as he replaced the receiver and lifted his medical bag.

'Ross Jordan. He's been crying half the night and now he's being sick. God, how I hate emergencies involving children.'

'Do you want me to come with you?'

'It's supposed to be your afternoon off,' he reminded her.

'So I can spend it how I choose,' she said winningly. 'Let's go.'

Pat Jordan looked completely exhausted when she opened the door to let them in.

'I'm sorry to be such a nuisance, Doctors,' she declared, leading the way into her sitting-room. 'My neighbour said Ross was probably just teething, but when he started being sick—'

'Don't apologise, Pat,' Bridie declared. 'We'd much rather be called out for a false alarm than have you not call us at all.'

Unfortunately it didn't look very much as though it were a false alarm. Ross was white-faced and pinched, and his tiny limbs were contorted in agony.

Jack examined him gently, his slender fingers probing over the child's small body, and then swiftly he removed his nappy. Bridie's heart sank. It looked as though it was full of redcurrant jelly.

'What is it? What's wrong?' Pat Jordan asked, her eyes large with fear as Jack took his cellphone from his bag and began to dial.

'It's an intussusception, Mrs Jordan,' he said, deliberately calm. 'Part of Ross's intestine has twisted round on itself, causing a blockage.'

'But that's curable, isn't it? I mean, it's not serious, is it?' Pat said tremulously.

'We need to get him into hospital right away—'

'You mean he might. . .he might—?'

'Where's your husband, Pat?' Bridie interrupted quickly.

'Dan's at the office, but—'

'Then why don't you phone him?' Bridie said soothingly. 'He'd want to know, you know he would.'

As Pat Jordan went to do as she suggested Bridie gazed at Jack worriedly. 'You're certain?'

Jack bit his lip as he cradled Ross in his arms. 'I can feel a solid lump on his abdomen. I'd like to be wrong but I don't think I am. I just wish she'd called us sooner—'

'Oh, be fair, Jack,' Bridie protested. 'Babies of that age cry a lot with wind, or because they're teething. Pat couldn't be expected to know it was this. I've only ever seen one other case in all my time in medicine.'

'I've seen two, and I hope to hell the ambulance comes quickly,' he said, his face dark. 'The interssusception is cutting off the blood supply to his intestines, and the longer it goes on the more likelihood there is he'll develop gangrene.'

'The hospital will do a barium enema prior to an X-ray, just to make sure of your diagnosis, and sometimes that moves the blockage without the need for surgery,' she declared, trying desperately to sound positive.

'And if it doesn't?' he replied bleakly. 'Look at him, Bridie. The little chap's exhausted. He's in no fit state for such a delicate operation.'

She gazed down at Ross. Jack was right. The operation was a difficult one at the best of times, without performing it on a child who had no physical reserves left.

'Could we try manual manipulation?' she suggested.

'Have you ever done it?' he asked, hope flickering in his eyes, only for it to die as she shook her head.

'I saw it done once when I was at medical school, and I know it's a tricky procedure, but surely it's worth a try?' she said insistently.

A deep furrow appeared on his forehead and then he shook his head. 'I don't have the skill—I wish I had, but I don't. What about you?'

She looked up at him uncertainly. It had been so long since she'd seen the procedure—what if she made the situation worse? What if she did more harm than good?

'If you think there's the remotest chance you can pull it off, do it, Bridie,' Jack said bluntly. 'He's in a bad way.'

She made up her mind. 'Put him on the floor.'

Quickly she got down on her knees beside Ross,

and gently but firmly put her fingers over his stomach. A small whimper came from him but he was too exhausted now even to cry any more. All he did was stare up at her, his large blue eyes registering pain, as gently—very gently—she began to knead the mass of tight intestine beneath her fingers, desperately trying to remember what she had seen the surgeon at medical school do.

For what seemed like hours but could only have been minutes nothing happened, and then gradually—very gradually—she felt a loosening. She scarcely dared breathe. She just kept on kneading, praying that the mass beneath her fingers would continue to shrink, and it did—to her complete amazement and joy it did.

'Well?' Jack murmured softly when she eventually leant back on her heels.

'I've done it,' she said in a daze. 'I don't know how, but I've done it.'

He hugged her tightly, his face suffused with such a blinding smile that she didn't know whether to laugh or cry.

'What is it, what's happened?' Pat Jordan exclaimed, wiping the tears from her cheeks with a trembling hand. 'Is. . .is he worse?'

'He's going to be all right, Mrs Jordan,' Jack declared, 'and it's all down to Dr McEwen. We still have to send Ross on to hospital, just to be on the safe side, but I can assure you he's going to be fine—just fine.'

And as though to prove the point Ross emitted a very loud burp and then chuckled.

'Do you want to go in the ambulance to the hospital, Bridie?' Jack asked as they heard it approaching the house.

She nodded. 'I won't stay long—I promise. Just long enough to see him settled.'

'Actually, I might follow you. You'll need a lift back—'

'Liar!' she laughed. 'I can get a taxi, as you well know. You're just as concerned as I am!'

'OK, OK, don't rub it in.' He grinned. 'Thanks for coming, Bridie,' he added. 'And thanks for what you did—that was one hell of a job.'

'I'm just relieved it worked,' she said. 'Most of the time I didn't have the faintest idea what I was doing.'

'Don't sell yourself short,' he said firmly. 'I know ability when I see it.'

She beamed up at him and went in the ambulance to the hospital, feeling quite ridiculously happy.

The consultant paediatrician at Perth confirmed that Bridie had indeed successfully manipulated the intussusception.

'Wonderful job, my dear,' he enthused. 'Couldn't have done it better myself. If you ever think of chucking in general practice get in touch. Hands like yours are hard to find. And now, you ignorant lot,' he continued, turning to a group of junior doctors who were clustered round him, 'I'll just explain exactly what Dr McEwen achieved this afternoon, for the benefit of those who didn't take it in the first time.'

'I think I might just sneak away, Jack,' Bridie whispered, red-cheeked with embarrassment as the consultant launched into yet another description of the procedure.

'Don't you want to bask in all this glory?' he chided, laughter plain in his brown eyes.

'Do I heck!' she muttered. 'I'll wait for you in the car.'

Jack waited only until Ross was safely settled into a ward and then, after a few encouraging words to his parents, he made his way to the exit, only to find Simon waiting for him.

'How's Bridie?' Simon said, his face unusually grim.

'A bit embarrassed by all this fuss, but pleased as Punch,' Jack said, smiling.

'Pleased? What, in God's name, has she to be pleased about?'

'Ross Jordan and his intussusception—'

'I'm not talking about that,' Simon broke in. 'I'm talking about Kirsty Ferguson.'

'Kirsty Ferguson?' Jack repeated, the smile dying on his face.

'I shouldn't have let her go,' Simon continued worriedly. 'She must have taken a taxi. I wouldn't have let her go if I'd thought she was just going to go home on her own—'

'What's happened, Simon?' Jack demanded.

'The Fergusons agreed to us switching off her life-support machine this morning. She died about three hours ago.'

Jack was already halfway down the stairs before Simon caught up with him and gripped him roughly by the shoulder.

'What does Bridie mean to you, Jack?'

Jack gazed at him in exasperation. 'What the hell kind of question is that to ask at a time like this?'

'A perfectly reasonable one, I would have thought,' Simon said evenly. 'She's upset right now, and I don't want you taking advantage of that. She's not. . .' He stopped, clearly searching for the right words. 'She's not the type of a woman for a casual relationship.'

'I don't need you to tell me that,' Jack replied through gritted teeth.

'Just as long as you remember it,' Simon said deliberately. 'I don't want her hurt by someone who is just passing through, and I won't *have* her hurt—do you understand me?'

Jack gazed at Simon with distaste. The man meant

well, he knew that, but right at that moment he would have liked nothing better than to punch the solicitous look off his face.

'I have to go,' he said with difficulty, and then, pulling himself free from Simon's restraining hand, took the remaining stairs in one.

'She's going to be very vulnerable,' Simon called after him. 'Remember that!'

Jack covered the distance between Perth Hospital and Struan at a speed Bridie would have been proud of, only to find the house in total darkness when he arrived.

Quickly he checked out the office and the consulting room, in case she'd had a call-out when she'd got back, but there was no note left for him on the bulletin board, no sign that she had been there at all. Her bedroom was empty, so too was the kitchen, and when he opened the sitting-room door and found that room in darkness too his concern began to deepen into real worry.

He turned, meaning to go downstairs again, and it was then that he heard it, a sigh so faint that it was scarcely more than a whisper on the air. He reached for the switch, and as light flooded the room he finally saw her, hunched in a corner of the sofa, her head in her hands.

She must have heard him for she looked up, her face white, her cheeks stained with tears.

'She's dead, Jack.'

'I'm so sorry, Bridie, so very sorry.'

She nodded blindly. 'She was just thirteen. She had all her life ahead of her, and now—'

He sat down and put his arm round her shoulder, and she leant against him wearily.

'I keep going over and over the day of her accident

in my mind,' she murmured. 'I keep thinking perhaps there was something else I could have done—something more I should have done.'

'There was nothing,' he said firmly.

'All those days of suffering for her and her parents,' she continued, as though he hadn't spoken. 'Why did we do it, Jack? Why did we try so hard to drag her back if it was only to end like this? We should just have let her slip quietly away.'

'Stop this!' he exclaimed, cupping her face deliberately in his hands, his eyes fierce. 'You're punishing yourself needlessly; you're crucifying yourself for doing your job. You did the best you could—I did the best I could—but it just wasn't enough. We're not gods, little one; we can't wave a magic wand and make things better just because we want it so badly.'

'I hear what you're saying,' she said raggedly, tears trickling down her cheeks, 'and I know you're right, but sometimes. . .oh, sometimes it's so hard.'

'Oh, Bridie, I'm not unfeeling; I'm not uncaring,' he said softly, wiping away her tears with his fingertips. 'But you must try and distance yourself. If you didn't you would never be able to go on.'

She nodded, and, because her eyes were brimming with unshed tears, because he wanted so desperately to comfort her, he bent his head and kissed her.

The touch of his lips was no more than the featherlight brushing of butterfly wings, and he released her immediately when he felt her move in his arms, but she wasn't moving away from him. Instead she turned fully towards him and tentatively reached up her hand to trace the outline of his jaw with her fingers.

He sat motionless, his heart thudding against his ribcage, as the gentle fingers moved from his jaw to his lips and then to smooth his hair back from his forehead. She gazed at him searchingly for a moment, and then to his complete surprise she tilted back her head and kissed him.

He would have had to be inhuman not to respond, not to deepen the kiss, not to wrap his arms around her and gather her to him, and he was not inhuman.

Dimly she heard him groan; dimly she was aware of his hands against her back—hands that were strong, hands that were powerful—but it was as though her body was no longer hers, as though it had suddenly acquired a mind and a will of its own. She seemed to be melting, floating on a sea of warmth—a warmth that began deep within her and then flooded out through her whole body.

She shivered slightly when she felt his tongue exploring her mouth, but it was not with panic, it was with exquisite pleasure, and suddenly she was responding to his insistent mouth with a fervour to match his own. As his lips left her mouth and caressed her throat her whole body seemed to leap and jerk towards him, and then suddenly he pulled back from her and stood up quickly.

'Jack?' Her face was bewildered, confused.

'I think we'd better stop right now before I forget all about my promise not to pressurise you,' he said hoarsely.

'But Jack—'

'Go to bed, Bridie. You need to sleep and I need—what I need is a good, long cold shower.' And before she could say anything he strode past her out of the room.

He let the cold water splash over his body for what seemed like an eternity before turning on the warm water. Simon was right. She was too vulnerable, too upset by Kirsty's death to know what she was doing. To have taken advantage now would have been unforgivable, and yet. . . Resolutely he crushed down the memory of her sweetness and softness and, wrapping a towel round his waist, he padded across to his bedroom, only to stop dead on the threshold.

His room was not empty. Bridie was sitting on the edge of his bed, dressed in a pair of faded striped pyjamas.

'Is there something wrong?' he asked, totally thrown.

She stood up. 'No, nothing. . .wrong. I've come. . . I've come because. . .I want you to make love to me. I know we have to. . .take precautions,' she added in a rush, hot colour flooding through her cheeks at his silence, 'so I got these from the surgery.'

She held out a small packet to him and he shook his head, not knowing whether to laugh or cry. She looked for all the world like a small child facing a gruelling visit to the dentist.

'Bridie, sweetheart, you don't have to do this; you don't have to prove anything—least of all to me,' he said gently. 'Now, come on, let's get you back to bed.'

He had her halfway to the door before she struggled free from his arm. 'Don't—oh, please don't send me away,' she entreated. 'I've been walking up and down my bedroom for the last half-hour trying to pluck up the courage to do this—'

He put his fingers to her lips. 'Oh, little one, making love isn't a test you have to endure, an examination you have to pass. Wait until you're sure this is really what you want—'

'If you send me away now I don't know when I'll have the courage to come back,' she said urgently, her eyes huge in her face. 'Please, Jack, I know what I'm doing. Please, please won't you help me?'

There was determination in her face, and yet there was a flicker of fear there too, and he knew that in all his life he had never less wanted to make love to a woman. If it all went wrong, if he couldn't conquer her fears, he knew that he would leave her feeling even more inadequate than she already did.

'Bridie, this isn't a good idea—'

'Don't. . .don't you want me any more?' she whispered.

He drew her into his arms and held her tightly, his throat constricted. 'Oh, Bridie, if only you knew how much,' he said huskily.

'Then help me; make love to me,' she murmured into his chest.

He could feel her whole body trembling, could feel her uncertainty, and he lifted her face to his. 'If I do, then I want you to promise me something. I want you to promise me that if I do anything you don't like you'll tell me. I want you to promise me that if I do something that frightens you you'll let me know immediately, and I want you to promise me—*promise* me,' he repeated insistently, 'that if you want me to stop you'll say so.'

She nodded, and gently he took her by the hand and led her towards the bed, but when he stretched out his hand towards the light switch she caught his hand.

'Please, can we leave it on? I need to know—I have to know—it's you.'

And he smiled understandingly and did as she asked. And then he made love to her.

Every touch was slow and overwhelmingly tender, each movement was at her pace, until he knew that her shuddering body no longer felt revulsion at the touch of his hand or the caress of his lips but only an overwhelming longing for that intimacy.

The small breasts that had recoiled from his fingers and mouth came to ache for their touch, the smooth thighs that had convulsed at his gentle stroking no longer screamed a protest but wanted—needed—a culmination. And at last, when he knew from her moist softness that she was never going to be any more ready than she was now, he entered her gently.

Only then did he see the flicker of panic in her eyes; only then did he feel her fingernails digging so deeply into his back that it was all he could do not to cry out.

'It's me, Bridie—not Cameron, not Lucy's father—it's me,' he said insistently, and heard her ragged sob as she clung to him.

There was no earth-shattering climax as his life-force surged within her, no roller coaster of mutual ecstasy—how could there be after so many years of doubt and fear?—and he knew that when he had moved within her she had felt little of the pleasure he had experienced, that he had left her body unfulfilled.

But when he cradled her in his arms and murmured softly into her hair, 'Next time, little one, next time it will be perfect,' tears trickled slowly down his cheeks as he heard her soft echo.

'Next time—yes, next time, Jack.'

CHAPTER EIGHT

'BRIDIE, wake up—you've got to get up!'

She opened her eyes slowly, focused for a second on the dark face gazing down at her, and then closed her eyes again with a groan. 'Have a heart, Jack. It's still night—'

'It isn't night,' he insisted. 'It's half past eight in the morning, and Fiona's going to be here at any minute.'

'Not funny, Jack.' She yawned, burying her head deep under the pillow. 'Now, please, let me go back to sleep.'

The pillow was yanked unceremoniously from her head and a clock was thrust into her face. She squinted at it sleepily, only to let out a shriek of dismay and then dive frantically beneath the bedclothes.

'Why didn't you wake me—why didn't you tell me the alarm had rung?' she called out in muffled accents from the depths of the bed.

'I forgot to set it,' he said ruefully as he pulled on his trousers. 'As you might recall, I had other things on my mind last night.'

She muttered something incoherent in reply and he lifted a corner of the bedclothes curiously. 'What, in God's name, are you looking for under there?'

'My pyjamas,' she cried, surfacing briefly. 'What's happened to my pyjamas?'

'Does it matter? Even Fiona's not nosy enough to check our beds.'

'But I can't get up without them,' she declared, considerably flustered. 'I've got nothing on.'

His lips twitched. 'From what I can remember, little

one, you've got absolutely nothing to be ashamed of.'

She blushed and smiled and got out of bed, only to blush even more furiously as his eyes travelled appreciatively over her. Quickly she made her way to the door, but she wasn't quick enough.

'You were right,' he murmured, gathering her to him. 'You should have put on your pyjamas. When you look like this the last thing I want you to do is get dressed.'

'Oh, Jack, Fiona will be here soon,' she protested as his fingers traced down her bare back, sending tiny shivers of pleasure coursing through her.

'She could be late this morning,' he observed, his mouth caressing her collar-bone and then travelling slowly downwards.

'And knowing Fiona she'll probably be early,' she sighed as her body arched in response to his gentle arousal, and sure enough, as though on cue, they both heard the sound of the front door opening and the patter of high heels on the hallway floor below.

'Do you think she's got the house bugged?' Jack exclaimed, his eyebrows rising comically, as Bridie disentangled herself from his arms and gazed at him in panic.

'What are we going to do?' she whispered. 'She always comes upstairs for a cup of coffee before morning surgery. She'll find us for sure.'

'How about if I say I was examining you—purely in the interests of medical science, of course?' he replied gravely, laughter plain in his eyes.

'It's not funny,' she hissed. 'You don't know Fiona like I do. She'll never let me hear the end of this if she finds out.'

'Then a strategic and very fast retreat is called for,' he declared. 'Shoot across to your room pronto, and I'll hold the fort as long as I can. Oh, and Bridie,' he added as she turned to go, 'you're wonderful—with or without clothes!'

She flashed him a radiant smile and fled.

She'd never dressed so fast in her life. Underwear, stockings and a blouse were dragged from the neat drawers they normally resided in; a skirt was equally ruthlessly pulled from its hanger. A quick wash in her bedroom sink, an even swifter brush through her tangle of curls, and she was ready.

She made for the bedroom door and then stopped—the bed. It was obvious that she hadn't slept in it last night, and though Jack might joke that even Fiona wasn't nosy enough to check on their sleeping arrangements she couldn't be certain of that.

She thumped at the pillows with her fist, rumpled the bedcovers, and then stood back to survey the result. An involuntary chuckle sprang to her lips. She'd overdone it a bit. Her bed looked as though she'd had a fight in it, but it couldn't be helped. Leaving Jack alone with Fiona for any length of time was not a good idea, and with that thought she strode purposefully across the hall and into the kitchen.

'Well, all I can say is the pair of you must be gluttons for punishment,' Fiona commented as soon as she saw her.

Bridie glanced at Jack in startled bewilderment.

'I was just telling Fiona we've been up for hours,' he declared, coming to her rescue quickly. 'We decided to have a go at clearing some of our paperwork, didn't we? Got up early, had breakfast a good couple of hours ago,' he added, his eyes drifting pointedly to the pristine kitchen table and empty sink.

'That's right,' Bridie nodded vigorously, accepting the cup of coffee Jack was holding out to her with relief, and hoping that the sound of her rumbling stomach was not as obvious to Fiona as it was to her.

'The early bird catches the worm, and all that sort of thing.'

'So you made quite an inroad into it?' Fiona observed. 'The paperwork, I mean?'

Bridie gazed at Jack in mute, panic-stricken appeal.

'Oh, we got through a fair amount,' he said airily.

'Really?' Fiona said thoughtfully, her eyes darting speculatively from Bridie to Jack, and then back to Bridie again. 'You'll need to let me see what you've done.'

'Has the mail come yet?' Bridie asked in strangled accents, glaring sideways at Jack. He'd really landed them in it now. It wouldn't take Fiona long to discover that the paperwork hadn't been touched.

'I've gone through it,' Fiona said as she handed it to her. 'Two letters from Perth Hospital, some circulars, and there's five applications for the post of locum—they're the ones at the bottom.'

Bridie took the letters from her. 'I'll read them later,' she said, as casually as she could. 'Could you open up the surgery for Jack and make out a list of the morning calls for me? We'll be down in a minute.'

Fiona nodded and made her way to the door, and Bridie sighed inwardly with relief, but her relief was destined to be short-lived. Just as Fiona was about to close the kitchen door behind her she turned, her expression gleeful.

'I know it's none of my business, but for people who have supposedly been up for hours you're a remarkably short-sighted pair,' she declared. 'Bridie—your blouse is buttoned up the wrong way, and Jack—your sweater's on inside out. Just thought I'd mention it before any of the patients see you.' And as she closed the door behind her the sound of her laughter drifted back to them.

Jack's face creased into a rueful grin. 'I think we've been rumbled.'

'I know we have,' Bridie sighed, rinsing her cup in the sink.

'Are you sorry?' he asked, coming up behind her and sliding his arms round her waist.

'If you mean about last night—absolutely not,' she said firmly, leaning back into his arms. 'If you mean about Fiona finding out—ask me that question again in a couple of days, after she's driven me crazy with her "I told you so" manner.'

He buried his face in the back of her neck and laughed. 'It's going to be a long day,' he murmured.

'Not if we work hard and think about something else.' She chuckled.

'Unfeeling slave-driver!'

'Realist, more like,' she returned with a smile. 'Now, you'd better get downstairs and start morning surgery before we have Fiona back up here again. The quicker we get started—'

'The quicker we'll be finished—I know,' he sighed. 'But don't work too hard, sweetheart. I'd like you to have plenty of energy left for tonight.'

Warm colour flooded through her cheeks and she dug her elbow lightly into his ribs. 'Will you go and start work, please?'

'OK, boss, anything you say, boss,' he declared, snapping to attention, and then completely ruining the effect by turning her round and kissing her lightly on the tip of her nose.

'You're an idiot, do you know that?' she called as he went out of the door.

'Does that mean you don't like me any more?' he shouted back.

'Exactly!' she returned, only to hear the sound of

his deep, throaty laughter as he clattered noisily down the stairs.

Her lips curved into a warm smile. She didn't just like him, she loved him, and she loved him with a depth and strength of feeling she hadn't known it was possible to possess. Before he came into her life she'd only been half living, and now. . .

She wrapped her arms round herself and closed her eyes as she remembered the touch of his lips and his hands on her body. Now everything was different; now the world was no longer a lonely place. Now there was Jack and she felt complete.

'Bridie, are you coming down for this list of morning calls some time this century?'

There was irritation as well as amusement in Fiona's voice, and Bridie frowned slightly. It sounded as though they had a busy morning ahead of them.

She lifted her medical bag from the table, only to send the morning mail scattering to the floor in her haste. With a sigh she bent and picked it up, and then extracted the ones from hopeful doctors applying for the post of locum.

'Sorry, boys.' She smiled as she put the letters into one of the kitchen drawers. 'There's no vacancy now.'

'At last!' Fiona declared when Bridie finally appeared in her office. 'I was just about to send out a search party for you. Now, here's your list of calls, and there's a late one in from Mrs Livingstone.'

'Elsa?' Bridie said with concern.

'She's not ill,' Fiona said quickly. 'She just phoned to say if you were anywhere near her cottage today she'd very much like you to pop in for a chat.'

Bridie drummed her fingers thoughtfully on the desk. 'And that's all she said?'

Fiona nodded.

'OK, I'll drop by after I've done my other calls,' Bridie replied, picking up the list of names and addresses that Fiona had typed for her. 'See you later.'

'Bridie.'

She turned, her eyebrows raised expectantly.

'Getting up early to do the paperwork suits you,' Fiona observed, her face perfectly serious, but her lips twitching slightly. 'I'd do more of it if I were you.'

'I intend to,' Bridie replied, equally serious, and went out of the door with Fiona's gale of laughter following her.

She was still smiling as she went about her rounds. Even Mrs Johnstone, who had the annoying habit of dragging out every member of her family for a consultation, failed to annoy her, and so did Mr Markham, who was never happy with anything she did. Nothing, it seemed, could bother her today; nothing could take away the secret joy that was wrapped around her heart.

'You're looking very chirpy this morning, Doctor,' Tom McDonald commented as she changed the dressings on his ulcerated leg.

'I feel chirpy, Tom,' she exclaimed. 'It's such a lovely day, don't you think?'

Tom gazed out at the heavy, leaden sky and then back at Bridie's glowing face, and smiled with understanding.

'What's up with you?' his wife observed as Bridie drove away. 'You're grinning like a Cheshire cat—Doctor given you good news, has she?'

'Indirectly,' he said mysteriously.

'What are you talking about, you daft old devil?'

'I just like to see folks happy, that's all,' he declared, returning deliberately to his jigsaw puzzle, leaving his wife to shake her head with exasperation and go back to the kitchen.

Tom smiled again as he tried to find the bit of blue

sky that would finish the top corner of his puzzle. It didn't need a degree to see which way the wind was blowing for young Dr McEwen, and why should he spoil her happiness by blabbing what he suspected? 'The local gossip-mongers will do that soon enough,' he sighed aloud.

It was only when Bridie approached Elsa Livingstone's small cottage that her spirits began to droop. Fiona had insisted that Elsa only wanted a chat, but Bridie wasn't convinced, and when she saw Elsa's split lip and the bruises round her throat that her scarf could not hide she could not prevent her exclamation of distress.

'Before you say a word, Doctor, wait until you hear what I have to say,' Elsa declared.

Bridie followed her through to her neat sitting-room, anger and impotence seething through her.

'I asked you to drop by, Doctor, because I'm leaving the area—'

'Leaving? But Elsa—'

'I said I wanted you to hear what I have to say, and you can't hear it if you keep interrupting, my dear,' Elsa said, smiling.

Bridie bit her lip ruefully. 'Sorry—go ahead.'

'You and Dr Culrain were right about Bill,' Elsa said awkwardly. 'He has no right to treat me the way he does and, before you ask—yes, he did do this to me,' she added, touching her throat and her lip. 'I knew it couldn't go on, but I didn't know what to do about it. I couldn't call the police and have him charged. No matter what you might think of him, Bill is still my son.'

Elsa lapsed into silence and Bridie waited, knowing how hard her admission had been for her.

'My daughter, Alice, arrived unexpectedly yesterday,' Elsa continued at last with an effort. 'Apparently a little bird phoned her and told her what was happening. Alice wouldn't tell me who the little bird was, only that it had a feminine voice and was concerned about me.'

Bridie studiously avoided Elsa Livingstone's eyes and the old lady chuckled. 'Don't worry, my dear, I shan't enquire into the identity of the little bird. All I want you to know is that Alice has asked me to come and stay with her in Edinburgh. She has a big house, she says, and she's going to convert part of it into a granny flat for me.'

'Oh, I'm so pleased, Elsa!' Bridie exclaimed with delight. 'But Bill—how is Bill going to react to this news?'

'We're not going to tell him,' Elsa replied. 'He's gone away for a few days' holiday with his friends, and won't be back until Tuesday and Alice has arranged for a removal van to take all of my furniture on Monday. The house will be put up for sale the next day.'

'You mean you're making him—?'

'Homeless?' Elsa nodded. 'Alice says it might bring him to his senses. I feel I should tell him what I'm doing, but Alice thinks not. She's worried he might. . .'

Her voice trailed away unhappily, and Bridie leant across and took her hands in hers.

'You're doing the right thing, Elsa,' she murmured. 'And I wish you all the happiness in the world.'

'Thank you, my dear,' Elsa replied, quite overcome. 'I'd wish you the same if I thought for one minute that you needed it, but from the bloom on your face this morning you don't.'

Bridie blushed and smiled.

'He's a fine young man, and handsome too,' Elsa observed, her lined face creasing into a smile. 'If I were forty years younger I'd be tempted to give you a run for your money.'

Bridie chuckled and followed Elsa to her front door. 'You'll keep in touch, won't you?' she urged. 'You'll let me know how you're getting on?'

'Of course.' Elsa smiled. 'I wouldn't forget my little bird, now, would I?'

'I'll hold you to that,' Bridie said firmly.

Elsa caught her hand. 'Thank you, my dear—for everything.'

'I'm just pleased it's all worked out for you,' Bridie replied, and then gasped in surprise as Elsa kissed her on the cheek. 'What was that for?'

'For being you,' Elsa said simply. 'Be happy, my dear—you deserve it.'

Bridie drove back to Struan, smiling. Everything seemed to be going right today. Even the world seemed more beautiful, or perhaps it was just her imagination. She'd always known that the countryside round Struan was lovely, but today it seemed sharper, clearer, more lovely than ever.

You're seeing the world through rose-tinted spectacles, Bridie McEwen, she told herself sharply, and then laughed out loud. What did she care if her spectacles were rose-tinted? She was happy, and that was all that mattered.

'Lovely day, Mrs Gibson, Mrs Howard,' she declared as she dropped into the corner shop to pick up some milk and eggs.

'I don't know about lovely. In fact, I'd say it was going to rain later,' Mrs Gibson replied dourly.

'Definitely rain.' Her friend Mrs Howard nodded knowledgeably. 'When you get clouds like that over the hill, rain's definitely on the way.'

'Well, I expect rain would be good for the gardens and the crops, wouldn't it?' Bridie beamed as she paid for her purchases and made her way back to her car.

'There's something different about that girl,' Mrs Gibson said, gazing thoughtfully after Bridie.

'She's wearing more modern clothes and she's changed her hairstyle,' Mrs Howard said helpfully. 'That makes a big difference to a girl.'

'Cobblers!'

The two women turned quickly to Jenny Simpson on the check-out till with affronted dignity.

'What kind of expression is that to use, Jenny Simpson?' Mrs Gibson announced. 'And, more to the point, what do you mean by it?'

'The doctor's in love.' Jenny smirked. 'It's as plain as the nose on my face.'

'In love?' Mrs Howard echoed, her eyebrows rising with keen interest. 'All right, then, Jenny Simpson, if you know so much about the doctor's private life who is she in love with?'

'Dr Culrain, of course.'

Mrs Howard looked at Mrs Gibson, and Mrs Gibson looked at Mrs Howard, and suddenly both ladies discovered that they had very pressing business to attend to, not least of which was to spread this very juicy titbit to everyone they met.

Blissfully unaware of the speculation surrounding her, Bridie parked her car outside her home and went inside, only to recognise a familiar voice emanating from Fiona's office.

'Andrew!' she exclaimed with delight, bending down to hug him warmly in his wheelchair. 'Why didn't you tell me you were coming? How are you? Can you stay long—?'

'Slow down, slow down!' He chuckled. 'I'm fine, as you can see. I just dropped in on the off chance, hoping to have a little chat with you and Jack.'

'Sounds ominous.' She smiled. 'Nothing wrong, I hope?'

'Not from my point of view, no,' he said.

'More and more mysterious,' she observed. 'What are you up to, Andrew?'

'Wait and see, my dear; wait and see. Jack, my boy, how are you?' he added as Jack came into the office.

'Fine, thank you, Andrew,' Jack declared, clasping Andrew's hand firmly in his while Bridie watched with a wide, satisfied smile.

Today *was* a special day, she thought as she made them all coffee and took it downstairs. She had the two men she loved most in all the world together in the same room, and she couldn't have been happier.

'So you're checking up on us, are you, Andrew?' Jack grinned as they sat round the table companionably.

'As if I would,' he declared. 'No, I've come for a very specific reason. I've decided I'm going to retire.'

'Oh, Andrew, no,' Bridie protested. 'You've years ahead—'

'There's no point in you trying to talk me out of it, Bridie,' he said firmly. 'I've made up my mind so the subject's not one for discussion. What *is* up for discussion is what's going to happen now. There are two things to consider,' he continued. 'The house and the practice. Now, as for the house, I know how fond you've grown of it, Bridie, so I'd like you to have the first option on it if you'd like.'

'If I'd like?' She beamed. 'Oh, Andrew, I'd like nothing better. I'll have to discuss it with the bank, of course, but I think they'll advance me the money.'

He nodded. 'And now for the second matter—the practice.'

Bridie smiled across at Jack, but to her surprise

he didn't smile back. If anything he appeared totally uninterested in the subject.

'You're going to need a new partner, Bridie,' Andrew continued. 'Locums are all very well for filling in temporarily, but they don't have the permanence our patients have a right to expect. Now, would either of you have any suggestions for my replacement?'

Bridie waited, certain that Jack would speak, certain that he would say that he would like nothing better than to join the practice permanently, but he didn't say anything; he simply stared down into the dregs of his coffee in silence.

Andrew glanced across at Bridie, his eyebrows raised questioningly, and she shook her head in bewilderment. She couldn't understand Jack's reticence at all.

'The kind of doctor I'm looking for,' Andrew continued, looking pointedly at Jack, 'is someone with a real feel for the place and the patients—someone who could complement and add to Bridie's skills.'

Still Jack said nothing, and a distinct feeling of unease began to creep into Bridie's heart—an unease she tried desperately to crush down. Perhaps Jack was just too embarrassed to push himself forward; perhaps he felt awkward suggesting himself for the post—yes, that must be it; that had to be it.

'Jack's done a first-rate job while you've been away, Andrew,' she said hurriedly. 'He gets on really well with the patients—better than I do at times.' She laughed and so did Andrew, but Jack, she noticed, did not. 'He would make an excellent partner if. . .if he wants it, that is,' she added, gazing at Jack and willing him to say something—anything.

'What about it, then, Jack, would you consider taking my place?' Andrew said at last, his manner jovial.

'No.' Jack's voice was low but his answer was clear

enough, and Bridie stared at him in disbelief.

How could he say no—after last night how could he possibly say no, just like that?

'Don't you want to think it over?' she floundered. 'I mean, give it some consideration, weigh up the pros and cons—'

'There's nothing to consider,' he said deliberately. 'Thanks for the offer, Andrew,' he continued, turning to him, 'but I'm afraid I'm just not interested.'

Andrew did not stay long after that. He said he was tired, that he had a long journey back to his sister's house, but Bridie knew he was merely being tactful.

'I thought Jack was settling in here,' Andrew said in confusion as he and Bridie waited outside for his taxi. 'I thought he'd jump at the chance to join the practice.'

'So did I,' she said bleakly.

'You've not had a row with him, have you?'

'No.'

Andrew shook his head. 'Then I don't understand—why won't he even consider it?'

'I don't know,' she replied, her throat so tight that it hurt.

'Have a word with him, my dear,' he said gently. 'See if you can make him change his mind. If you can't, we'll have to start looking for someone else—and fast. The last thing I want is you soldiering on with a series of locums—it's not good for the patients.'

She nodded.

'Are you all right, my dear? You look a bit pale.'

'I'm fine—just fine,' she said with an effort. 'Here's your taxi, Andrew.'

Once she and the taxi-driver had helped him in, he rolled down the window, his kindly face concerned. 'Look, I'm sorry about this—really sorry. I thought you and Jack—'

'Don't keep the taxi waiting, Andrew—they cost enough as it is.'

He patted her hand understandingly. 'I'll be in touch, my dear.'

Slowly she went back into the house. She had been so sure that Jack would want to join her in the practice—after last night what else was she supposed to think? That it was nothing more than a one-night stand, a little voice whispered, and a half-sob broke from her. Was that all it had meant to him, was that really all?

She forced herself to think back, to remember what he had said when he'd held her in his arms, to recall what he'd whispered when he'd made love to her. He hadn't said that he loved her. He'd said that he cared for her, he'd said that he wanted her, but he'd never said that he loved her.

She clutched at the banister, desperately trying to pull herself together. She had to brazen this out; somehow she had to brazen it out. Her heart was breaking, but Jack must never know how she felt. If she could take nothing else out of this mess then at least she wanted to hold onto her self-respect.

'He's looking really well—Andrew,' Jack declared as she came into the kitchen.

'Isn't he?' she agreed brightly. 'Do you want another coffee?' she continued. 'I'm having one—'

'Bridie, you knew my being here was only temporary,' he interrupted. 'I have a job lined up in the States—a good job. I never intended staying on in Britain.'

'Fine,' she said abruptly, busying herself with filling the kettle.

'Will you leave that alone and listen to me?' he demanded, spinning her round towards him. 'I want you to understand—really understand. It isn't you, or Struan; it's just that I know from experience that nothing ever lasts with me. I start a new job, full of enthusiasm, and then the enthusiasm wanes. I meet a new girl and I'm interested in her for a while, and then the interest fades. I've a lousy track record, Bridie. Every time I've thought, Maybe this is a place where I can be happy, it's never worked out.'

'It's nothing personal—is that what you're saying?' she said, as evenly as she could, unbelievably hurt that he could imply that he was bored with her already. 'So long, Bridie, it's been nice to know you—is that it?'

He winced. 'You make it sound so cold-blooded.'

'I'm sorry,' she said flatly. 'I'm sure there's an accepted dialogue for occasions like this, but I haven't had much practice, you see.'

'Oh, Bridie, you've been so lucky in your life—'

'Lucky?' she gasped. 'You think my life has been *lucky*!'

He bit his lip. 'I meant in terms of having good friends, of finding a place where you can be contented, of having the love of a parent. I've never had any of that.'

'But just because things have gone wrong for you in the past doesn't mean they always have to,' she insisted. 'Perhaps if you stopped being so cynical and learned to trust. . .' She came to a halt as he shook his head, his eyes bitter.

'Do you know what the word "love" means to me, Bridie?' he said, his face twisting slightly. 'It means pain and heartache. It means watching my parents withhold love for a punishment, or promise it like a carrot, a bribe to get what they wanted, with me stuck in the middle desperately trying to catch the crumbs.

'It's a meaningless word I've whispered to a woman I've held in the dark of the night, a word she's whispered back, with both of us knowing we'd be handing out the same line to someone else in a few weeks' time.

'It's an emotion I know nothing about, an emotion I don't trust, and an emotion I can't give. That's why it's best we end it now, before you fall in love with me. I don't want you hurt, you see, and I know that if I stay on you will be eventually.'

But it's already too late, her heart cried out; I've already fallen in love with you, and I'm already hurt. But she didn't say that. Instead she gripped the edge of the table tightly. 'So you're going to America.' It wasn't a question, just a statement.

'Yes, I'm going to America.'

'What happens now? Do we shake hands and part as friends—is that the routine?' she observed, and when he nodded she smiled crookedly. 'There, you see, Jack? I'm a quick learner.'

'Bridie—'

'Don't worry about the practice,' she continued quickly, reaching for the kitchen drawer and pulling out the letters she had put in there that morning. 'Look—there's five replies already to my advertisement for a locum, and I'm sure at least a couple of them must be good enough to be offered a partnership.'

'You'll be all right?' he said uncertainly. 'When I'm gone, I mean?'

'Of course!' she exclaimed in apparent surprise. 'I don't. . .need you to stay. The practice will survive, and as for me—hey, look at me; I'm all cured. You know, I don't think I ever did thank you properly for the miracle cure, did I?' she continued with a desperate brightness, though the ache in her chest was so acute that it was like a physical pain. 'You should consider specialising in it—sex therapy for women with problems—'

'Bridie, don't do this,' he said, moving towards her, his face tender.

'Don't do what?' she exclaimed. 'Goodness, you

should see your face.' She laughed, and if the laughter sounded a little brittle to her own ears he didn't seem to notice it. 'Why so glum? Aren't you pleased with your success? I thought this was what you wanted—to see me independent, not clinging to you. Well, I am independent, Jack—completely.'

'I will always remember you as a very special lady,' he said softly.

His words were like a knife in her heart, more hurtful than if he'd said she meant nothing at all to him, and her mouth tightened. 'I must make a start on answering these application letters. You'll be gone soon, and Andrew wants it all sorted out as quickly as possible.'

Without looking at him she walked briskly to the door, though her legs felt like lead.

'Bridie—'

She didn't—couldn't—turn round. 'Yes?'

'I just want you to be happy, little one,' he murmured.

She supposed that she mumbled something in reply but she didn't know what. All she knew was that she had to get away from him, to be by herself, not to see him again until the hard lump in her throat had subsided.

Quickly she went down to her consulting room and closed the door behind her. Determinedly she sat down at her desk and took the neatly typed letters out of their envelopes. But as qualifications mingled with addresses, and addresses merged into 'what my interests are', she found herself staring, unseeing, at the wall, wanting to cry. But no tears would come, and somehow that was the worst thing of all.

CHAPTER NINE

'It's a dreadful shame Dr Culrain's leaving us, isn't it, Doctor?'

Mrs Findlay's face was bland, but her beady eyes were sparkling with speculation and Bridie smiled tightly and stared deliberately at the blood-pressure gauge.

'He's been such an asset to the practice, don't you think?' Mrs Findlay continued. 'And everyone likes him.'

'Your blood pressure seems perfectly normal, Mrs Findlay—'

'I just can't help thinking it's a strange decision on his part, what with you and him seeming to get on so well, and Dr Weston retiring and all.'

Mrs Findlay's observation hung in the air, pregnant with meaning, and Bridie widened her smile with difficulty. 'There was never any question of Dr Culrain staying here permanently, Mrs Findlay,' she said evenly. 'He had already accepted a post in America.'

'But I thought you and he—'

'I think I'll arrange for you to have a barium enema examination, Mrs Findlay,' Bridie said quickly. 'There's no cause for alarm,' she added as Mrs Findlay's jaw dropped appreciably, 'but it's best to check out every avenue, don't you think?' And a barium enema is just about the most uncomfortable thing I can legitimately arrange for you to have done, you nosy old witch, she thought savagely.

'That's the last of the patients, thank God,' Fiona declared after Mrs Findlay had gone. 'It's been really busy these last few days and I can't think why.'

Bridie could, only too clearly. Quite where and how the rumours had started she couldn't even begin to guess, but somehow the entire community seemed to know that she was in love with Jack, and once word had got about that he was leaving the surgery had been inundated with patients who hadn't been there for years—patients whose expressions were sympathetic, or curious, or just plain knowing.

'Look, Bridie, I know it's none of my business,' Fiona continued uncertainly as she replaced some files in the filing cabinet, 'but just what are you up to?'

'I'm bringing these case notes up to date.'

'That's not what I meant, and you know it,' Fiona replied, shutting the filing cabinet with a bang.

'And, if I don't, you're going to enlighten me, aren't you?' Bridie said, putting down her pen with a smile.

Fiona gazed at her with clear exasperation. 'How can you be so. . .so damned cheerful all the time? Jack's leaving in a week and you're going round like some demented Mary Poppins, laughing and joking—it's driving me crazy!'

'What would you rather I do—go into deepest mourning?' Bridie said evenly. 'He was a temporary locum; he's fulfilled his contract; he's leaving—end of story.'

'I don't know how you can be so—'

'Hard?'

'Not hard, exactly.' Fiona frowned. 'Indifferent—that's the word I'm searching for—indifferent. I thought you liked him—more than liked him—'

'So?'

'The way you're treating him—'

'You mean I'm ignoring him?'

'No, I don't mean that.'

'You mean I'm being rude to him?'

'I wish you were—at least that would be more normal!' Fiona exclaimed.

'So what you're saying is you'd be happier if I either went into a decline or tore him off a strip?'

'Yes—no—oh, I don't know,' Fiona declared. 'All I do know is that your Mary-Poppins act isn't half wearing me down.'

Bridie laughed and shook her head, and Fiona banged out of the door in a temper.

Resolutely Bridie picked up her pen and went back to the case notes, but her interest in them was gone and eventually she threw aside her pen with a sigh.

Fiona was wrong. She was anything but indifferent to the situation. She cared desperately that Jack was leaving, but the only way she could cope was by pretending that she didn't, and being constantly cheerful was her only shield.

Everywhere she went she was sure that she saw sympathy in her patients' eyes, could even imagine their whispered comments—'Isn't it sad about Dr McEwen? She's in love with that Dr Culrain but it hasn't worked out for her, poor girl.'

She closed her eyes tightly. The last thing she wanted was anyone's pity; the last thing she could take at the moment was people feeling sorry for her.

'What a bloody morning,' Jack declared, striding into the consulting room without warning. 'Old Mr Gibson doesn't have flu, he's got pneumonia—and badly. I waited until the ambulance came but I think it's going to be touch and go whether he makes it.'

'The Gibsons have always been reluctant to face up to illness,' she said with an effort. 'They both hate hospitals and will do anything to avoid them.'

'Well, if Mr Gibson's lucky enough to pull through this he's going to have plenty of time to get used to being in one.'

He sat down opposite her and began going through the calls he'd made that morning, but he could have been talking double Dutch for all she knew. All she could think about was how attractive he was—how devastatingly attractive.

Her features might be schooled into apparently rapt attention as he outlined the treatments he had prescribed for various patients, but her eyes were tracing the firm outline of his jaw and the gentle curve of his lips. Far from concentrating on patients, she was imagining smoothing back the black hair that fell across his forehead and remembering the dark hair that had curled on his chest and the hard muscle of his thighs against hers. . .

'So I thought a course of penicillin might do the trick. What do you think?'

He was gazing at her with a quizzical smile, and she felt hot colour creeping up her neck. Who on earth was he talking about? The smile on his lips deepened and she got to her feet quickly. Surely, oh, surely he wasn't able to read her mind?

'I think that as you saw the patient it must be your decision. . .' she began. 'Oh, Fiona, coffee—great,' she added with ill-disguised relief.

'What time is this Dr Martin due to arrive?' Fiona asked as she handed round the coffee and helped herself to a biscuit.

'Any time now,' Bridie replied.

'Well, I hope he's a lot more promising than the last two doctors you've interviewed have been.' Fiona grimaced. 'Talk about hopeless! That tall, lanky one—'

'Dr Edwards?'

'Yes, him—he went around with his nose in the air the whole time, saying, "It's not quite Edinburgh or Glasgow, is it?" What did he expect? This is the country, for heaven's sake. And as for the little dumpy one—'

'Dr Gordon.'

'Whatever,' Fiona continued dismissively. 'He said, "Wonderful, wonderful," so many times I wanted to scream!'

'They both had excellent qualifications,' Bridie observed tightly, well aware that Jack was listening with keen interest.

'As locums, perhaps,' Fiona replied, taking a bite out of her biscuit thoughtfully, 'but neither were partner material, surely?'

'I thought Dr Gordon had the makings of an excellent partner,' Bridie said coolly. It was a downright lie—he would have driven her mad in less than a week—but not for one moment was she going to admit it, with Jack sitting there regarding her so intently.

'Each to his—or her—own opinion, I suppose,' Fiona declared. 'Oh, by the way, Jack, this came for you when you were out on your rounds,' she added, holding out a letter to him. 'It's got an American postage stamp on it—must be details of your new job.'

He took it from her without comment, and to her clear disappointment pushed it unopened into his jacket pocket. 'I suppose I'd better get back to my typing,' she continued, glancing from Jack to Bridie, clearly hoping that one of them would detain her.

'Fine,' Bridie observed. 'Give me a buzz when Dr Martin gets here, will you?'

Fiona opened her mouth and then closed it again and went back to her office, muttering something unintelligible under her breath.

'Did I hear you say to Fiona at breakfast that you were going over to Perth Hospital later?' Jack commented when they were alone.

'Simon wants me to have a word with Mary

Robinson,' she replied. 'She's refusing to have her hysterectomy and he's hoping I can persuade her to change her mind.'

'I thought she was really keen to have the op?'

'She was until some doom-and-gloom merchant got hold of her and told her the op was excruciatingly painful, that she'd get fat afterwards, and that women who'd had hysterectomies aged prematurely.'

He shook his head angrily. 'Why can't these people keep their mouths shut? The technique's changed out of all recognition since the early days, when women looked as though they'd been stitched together with fishing line and metal clamps.

'She'll have a little discomfort, certainly, but any weight she puts on will be because she's eating too much, and as for ageing more rapidly—hormone replacement therapy will solve that problem.'

She nodded, and an awkward silence descended over the consulting room—a silence she couldn't have broken to save herself. The letter Jack had received from America made everything seem so final, so irrevocable, and it was with relief that she saw him finally get to his feet.

'This Dr Martin you're interviewing this afternoon,' he said casually. 'Does he seem a likely candidate?'

'On paper he sounds perfect,' she replied, deliberately enthusiastic. 'Excellent qualifications, and he's had a fair bit of experience, too.'

'If he's that damn good why's he not in a practice already?' he replied disparagingly.

'He's been in Africa for the last three years, working in a missionary hospital.'

'Oh.' He looked momentarily disconcerted, and then rallied. 'I hardly think missionary medicine is going to be very useful in a Scottish practice.'

'I don't see why not,' she said smoothly as the front

doorbell rang. 'And anyway, I've learned not to make snap judgements about anything—or anyone.'

'Yes, but a medical missionary, Bridie—'

The buzz of the intercom silenced him.

'Dr Martin to see you, Brid—Dr McEwen.'

'Send him in, Fiona.'

Fiona went one better. She ushered Dr Martin in herself, and it took all of Bridie's self-control not to laugh out loud as her receptionist gave a very definite thumbs-up sign behind his back. He was certainly good-looking—blond hair, grey eyes, and a wide smile—but if Fiona was impressed Jack was clearly anything but. The frown-line between his black brows deepened considerably.

'You can get back to your work now, Fiona,' she said as her receptionist hovered eagerly in the background. 'And I'm sure you've got things to do too, Dr Culrain,' she added deliberately.

It was hard to tell who was most reluctant to leave—Jack or Fiona—but eventually they both went and she was able to conduct the interview alone as she had wanted.

Will Martin was by far the best candidate she had seen yet. His CV was excellent, his attitude was good and, most importantly from Bridie's point of view, he was engaged to a dental nurse whose picture he was only too delighted to pull out of his wallet for her approval. Unfortunately it was the fiancée who presented the main stumbling block to his taking up the post.

'I understood it was a locum you were looking for, not a permanent partner,' he said regretfully. 'When Maggie and I came back to Britain I promised I would try and get a practice near her parents—they're getting on in years, you see, and she wants to be near them.

'I only applied for this post because I thought it would be an ideal way of easing myself back into British medicine again. I never expected to be offered a partnership.'

'Where exactly do your fiancée's parents live?'

'Dundee.'

Bridie sighed. 'That's hardly a hop and a skip from Struan.'

'I'm really sorry about this, Dr McEwen—I seem to have wasted your time.'

'It isn't your fault—and please call me Bridie,' she declared, with a smile. 'When I placed that advertisement I *was* only looking for a locum, but circumstances have changed since then. Why don't you have a chat with your fiancée, see if you can't get her to change her mind?'

He nodded, but she could tell from his expression that it was unlikely. Despite this she dutifully spent the next hour and a half explaining how the practice ran, the range of patients they had, and the difficulties they encountered being in such a rural area. Will Martin in turn told her of his experiences in Africa, and because he had a ready wit and an acute sense of the ridiculous he soon had her laughing at his stories.

'I'm really pleased to have met you, Will,' she declared truthfully as she walked with him to the front door.

'Likewise, Bridie,' he replied. 'And I'll be in touch as quickly as I can.'

'With good news, I hope.' She smiled, well aware that the door to Fiona's office was ajar and that there was a very definite shadow at the top of the stairs.

Fiona flew out of her office as soon as Will Martin had gone, and Jack's descent down the stairs was no less rapid.

'Now, that's what I call a doctor,' Fiona observed

approvingly. 'He's a real cutey, Bridie.'

'He's certainly well qualified—'

'Oh, to hell with his qualifications.' Fiona giggled. 'He could examine me any day of the week.'

Bridie chuckled and lifted her medical bag.

'Can I have a word, Bridie?'

She glanced at her watch with a frown. 'Can't it wait, Jack? I promised I would see Mary Robinson—'

'This will only take a minute.'

She put down her bag reluctantly and followed him back into the consulting room.

'Look, it's about my replacement.' He paused, looking distinctly awkward and ill at ease, but she simply stared back at him, refusing to come to his rescue. 'I just thought that if you're having difficulty finding a replacement for me I could ask my employers in the States to hold my appointment for another month,' he continued at last. 'It would give you longer to look around for the right doctor.'

Anger flooded through her. Was she supposed to feel grateful for his sacrifice? Was she supposed to fall at his feet and say, 'Oh, thank you, Jack; I don't know what I'd do without you, Jack'?

'There's absolutely no need for that,' she said, as calmly as she could. 'Will Martin seems ideal—'

'You're surely not seriously thinking of asking him to join the practice, are you?' he exclaimed. 'He's totally unsuitable.'

She could have told him it was highly unlikely that Will Martin would be able to accept the post, that at the moment it looked very much as though she was going to have to ask Bob Maxwell over at Pitagowan to help her out for a while, but even if she'd been forced to walk over hot coals she wouldn't have told him that. Something about his manner had got under her skin, and she was damned if she was going to let him see that she couldn't manage without him.

'As far as I could tell, Will Martin is just about perfect,' she said stiffly.

'He's completely the wrong type for the practice,' he snapped.

'Oh? And what would you consider to be the right type—for the practice?' she asked, her colour beginning to rise.

'Someone older, more settled. Someone with a wife and family, not—'

'Not someone tall and good-looking?' she suggested.

'That's not what I meant—'

'No? But you'd be happier if he were fat and bald and with four kids, is that it?'

'I am merely attempting to help you make a professional, impartial judgement,' he retorted, his colour almost as high as hers.

'Oh, really?' she said drily. 'Well, thanks for the advice, Jack; I'll bear it in mind.'

She walked quickly out to the hall, only to discover that he had followed her.

'You're doing this just to annoy me, aren't you?' he declared angrily. 'You're deliberately picking the worst possible candidate—'

'I'm doing *what*?' she gasped, swinging round on him. 'My God, when it comes to egos yours certainly takes some beating!'

'I have a right to an opinion, and so does Andrew—'

'No, you don't—neither of you do,' she snapped. 'This has got nothing to do with Andrew and it sure as hell has got nothing to do with you. Andrew's retiring and you're going to be living on the other side of the Atlantic—the decision is mine and mine alone.'

He stared at her silently for a moment, and then his face set into harsh lines. 'All right, you've made your point—it's none of my business.'

'Good—I'm glad we've got that sorted out,' she retorted, and slammed out of the house.

His face set into even harsher lines as he heard the screech of her brakes when she raced out of the driveway. For a moment he stood indecisively in the hall and then, after a few choice and pithy words to Fiona, who had unwisely chosen to pop her head round her office door, he strode back into the consulting room and banged the door shut with a force that more than matched Bridie's.

He'd only been trying to be helpful, for God's sake, he thought belligerently as he threw himself down in her chair. And what had happened? She'd bitten his head off for his pains. Well, on her own neck be it, he decided resentfully. If she was stupid enough to choose someone who looked like some third-rate Greek statue come to life she had only herself to blame.

He pulled out the letter that Fiona had given him and tried to read it, but no matter how hard he concentrated the words just didn't seem to make any sense. All he could see was a wealth of copper-coloured hair and a pair of large, heather-coloured eyes; all he could picture was a soft body clinging to his, with a gentle voice whispering, 'Next time—yes, next time, Jack.'

He groaned out loud. What, in God's name, was the matter with him? He should have been looking forward to leaving, to the challenge of a new job, but he wasn't looking forward to it. He should have been pleased that Bridie seemed to be handling his departure so well, but he wasn't pleased. He was piqued by her cheerfulness—damnation, he wasn't just piqued, he was furious. At the very least he would have thought that she could be just a little sorry to see him go, but he'd heard her this afternoon laughing and joking with Will Martin.

Unconsciously he crushed the letter from America between his fingers. He had Will Martin's measure, that was for sure. Already he had managed to ingratiate himself into Bridie's good books. Once he was living here. . .

He got to his feet quickly and went across to the office. 'If anyone's looking for me, Fiona, I'll be at Perth.'

'But why are you going to—?'

The bang of the front door was her only answer, and Fiona sighed and returned to her typing and found herself wondering why on earth she had ever wanted to become a medical receptionist in the first place.

Tuesdays were always particularly busy at Perth Hospital. It was the day when patients were normally admitted in preparation for their operations, and by the time Jack had pushed his way through the collection of relatives who had accompanied their loved ones, and had made his way to Women's Surgical, it was to discover that Bridie had already left.

'It turned out to be a storm in a teacup,' the ward sister explained, her face distinctly harassed as she directed patients to their beds. 'Mrs Robinson's husband came in and he persuaded her to have the op. I meant to phone Dr McEwen to tell her she needn't come, but as you can see for yourself,' she added, with an expressive sweep of her hand at the mêlée of patients, 'it's bedlam in here.'

'Do you know whether Dr McEwen intended going straight home?'

'I think she was going to have a word with Dr Morrison first,' the sister replied vaguely, 'but I can't say for sure. No, you can't choose which bed you have, Mrs Denton,' she continued with exasperation as a large lady in an impressive straw hat collared her. 'This isn't a hotel, you know.'

Jack threw the ward sister a look of sympathy and made his escape, but as he walked quickly along the corridor to where Simon had his office a vaguely familiar young doctor called on him to stop.

'Neil Jardine,' the doctor explained tactfully, when Jack gazed at him with puzzlement. 'We met after you had that rather spectacular scene with our ice maiden in the hospital canteen.'

'I remember you now,' Jack replied, his face tightening. 'You're the junior doctor with the big mouth.'

Neil looked momentarily disconcerted, and then smiled. 'I have to say we never thought you'd pull it off. Many men have tried to thaw out Bridie McEwen and none have succeeded until you—and you must have succeeded, judging by the transformation in her.'

Jack threw him a look of disdain and tried to walk on, but Neil Jardine barred his way.

'As I told you at the time, we've been running this sweepstake for quite a few years now and it's accumulated to a tidy sum—three hundred pounds in all—and it's all yours if you can confirm you got her into bed.'

Anger flooded through Jack—cold, furious anger—and he lunged at Neil, only to stop short in horror. Over the top of Neil's head he could see Bridie at the far end of the corridor, and she had all too plainly heard every word. She was staring at him, her face stricken with pain, her eyes filled with hurt.

'Can you confirm it, Dr Culrain?' Neil continued. 'We can make out a cheque—'

'Get out of my way!' Jack said dangerously.

'But the cheque—'

'Get out of my bloody way!' he repeated, but when he finally obeyed Jack groaned out loud.

The corridor was empty. Only the gently swinging

door showed that there had ever been anyone there, and he turned on Neil with such fury in his face that the junior doctor backed away rapidly. 'Look, if you'd rather have cash, Dr Culrain—'

The next thing Neil Jardine knew was that he was travelling at speed towards the wall, the lapels of his white coat caught in a vice-like grip.

'Now, hear me, and hear me good,' Jack said through clenched teeth. 'Your betting activities on the subject of Dr McEwen's private life stop here. It's demeaning and degrading, and more befitting a group of schoolboys than members of the medical profession.'

'Hey, it was just a joke—' Neil began, only to subside into silence at the look in Jack's eyes.

'I'd punch you senseless if I thought it would do a damn bit of good, but you're not worth it—you're not even bloody worth it,' Jack said, releasing him with distaste.

'I promise you one thing, however,' he added as Neil pulled his coat down with a shaking hand. 'If I hear a whisper of this outside the hospital—even the merest suspicion of a whisper—I'll come back and I'll break every bone in your body. Do you hear me?'

'I hear you.' Neil nodded vigorously and fled.

Bridie never quite knew how she got home that day—she supposed she must have driven on autopilot. It was only when she drew up outside her home that the thoughts she had been trying so hard to subdue came flooding back, and she leant her head against the steering wheel wretchedly.

She'd thought she had plumbed the depths of misery when she'd learned that she had meant no more to Jack than a simple one-night stand, but to know that he had made love to her for a bet was the ultimate humiliation.

How was she ever going to be able to face the staff at the hospital again? How was she ever going to be able to talk to them normally? They must all be laughing at her behind her back, sniggering in corners.

When Jack had got so angry about Will Martin she had hoped. . . What had she hoped? That he would say that he didn't want Will because he was jealous of him, that he didn't want to go because he loved her?

A bitter smile appeared on her face. All he'd said was that it was none of his business. Forget him, Bridie, she told herself; chalk it up to experience. But how could she when she felt as though her world was falling apart?

Wearily she got out of the car, only to pause. There was a light on in the consulting room. Fiona must either be working late or she had forgotten to switch it off before she went home. With a sigh she went into the house, steeling herself to meet her receptionist, but it wasn't Fiona in the consulting room, it was Bill Livingstone.

'I'm sorry, but there's no evening surgery tonight, Bill,' she said, unaccountably unnerved. 'If you want to make an appointment—'

'I don't want an appointment, you stuck-up bitch,' he declared, lurching towards her and knocking a pile of folders from the desk as he did so. 'I want to talk to you.'

She gazed up at him uncertainly. He was a big man—a very big man—and he had been drinking and was drinking still. 'It's late, Bill,' she said, with a calmness she was very far from feeling. 'Why don't you come back tomorrow—?'

'You're a cow—do you know that?—a bloody interfering cow!' he snarled. 'It's all your fault—my mum going off like that. If you hadn't stuck your nose in where it wasn't wanted we'd be all right.'

'I can understand your anger, Bill, but this isn't getting us anywhere,' she said, edging slowly towards the door, only to stop as he slipped between her and it with amazing speed.

'Oh, no, you don't.' He laughed, banging the door shut. 'You're not getting away from me as easy as that.'

She backed away from him, real fear gripping her. 'Why don't you sit down? We could talk about this calmly.'

'"Why don't you sit down? We could talk about this calmly,"' he mimicked. 'It's all right for you, isn't it? You've got this big, fancy house—but me, I'm homeless now because of you, and I tell you this—you're not going to get away with it; you're not bleeding well going to get away with it!'

His hand came up and she ducked just in time as his half-empty bottle of whisky flew past her head, shattering against the wall behind her, and then he began to advance towards her, murder plain in his face. Terrified, she started throwing anything and everything she could lay her hands on at him—books, case files, specimen jars—but still he came towards her, and in desperation she picked up the letter opener from her desk.

'I'll use this—if you lay one finger on me, I swear to God I'll use it!' she cried, and then gasped with relief as a familiar voice rang out.

'Why not try picking on someone your own size, Bill?'

Bill turned unsteadily on his feet towards the newcomer; there was the harsh sound of knuckle hitting cheek-bone, and he went down like a stone.

'Are you all right, Bridie?' Jack asked urgently, coming across to her quickly, rubbing his grazed knuckles. 'Did that bastard hurt you?'

She shook her head, but her knees were trembling

so much that she had to grip the edge of the desk for support.

He searched her face. 'You're sure you're all right—he didn't. . .he didn't touch you?'

'I'm fine, honestly,' she managed to say. 'I'm just so very glad you came.'

'Hey, didn't you know that my middle name was Galahad?' He grinned. She tried to smile but a half-sob broke from her, and he put a comforting arm round her shoulder and then salvaged the phone from the floor.

'Oh, Jack, don't call the police,' she begged. 'It would kill Elsa if her son ended up in court.'

'And Bill Livingstone could have killed you,' he protested. 'He's dangerous, Bridie. If you won't think of yourself, think of the other women in the village. What if he tries these bully-boy tactics on one of them?'

She gazed at Bill Livingstone's inert form. Jack was right. She couldn't ignore what had happened, no matter how much it would hurt Elsa.

'All right, phone them,' she said reluctantly.

The police were there within minutes. Statements were taken, Bill Livingstone was led away to the car, and Sergeant Wilson and his constable drove off, siren wailing unnecessarily, clearly delighted to have been able to make an arrest in a village not noted for its crime levels.

'That should set tongues wagging in the village,' Jack chuckled, and then could have bitten off his tongue when he saw the pain that his casual words had evoked. 'What you heard at the hospital, Bridie—'

She walked deliberately towards the door and he caught her arm quickly. 'Don't you dare walk away from me!' he exclaimed. 'I won't have you condemn me without a hearing!'

'Go to hell!' she spat back at him.

He pulled her to him angrily, and suddenly he was

kissing her, his lips insistent, demanding, his body hard against hers. Her lips opened traitorously, revelling in the contact of his tongue, in the sensations the touch of his hands was kindling deep within her.

He wasn't being gentle and neither was she. It was almost as though they were both punishing one another, but she didn't care. She wanted him. Every part of her was responding with a desperate urgency to match his own—every part except her mind. Her mind could not forget what she had heard at the hospital, and she dragged herself out of his arms, her breathing ragged, her eyes hard.

'I didn't realise the stakes were higher if you got me to do a repeat performance, Jack.'

He could not have flinched more if she'd actually hit him.

'That's a terrible thing to say,' he said hoarsely.

'I'm a novice in the subtleties of situations like this, remember?' she said, her voice devoid of all emotion. 'What am I supposed to do—laugh it off, be flattered?'

'You can't—you surely can't believe that I would make love to you for a bet?'

The horror in his voice sounded genuine enough, but she gazed at him impassively for a moment and then she shook her head. 'I don't know, Jack. That's the trouble, you see—I honestly don't know.' And she went out of the door without a backward glance.

He didn't try to stop her this time; there seemed little point. He stood instead amongst the wreckage in the consulting room and then abstractedly began to pick up the pieces of broken glass.

Now he knew why he didn't want to leave; now he knew why he had been so angry at her apparent indifference. He was in love with her. For the first time in his life he was in love, and he'd discovered it too late.

CHAPTER TEN

'BILLS, more bills, letters from Perth Hospital,' Fiona commented as she flicked through the morning mail. 'Oh, and there's a postcard from Elsa Livingstone—lovely picture of Edinburgh Castle on the front. She says she's settling in well with her daughter and quite understands why you decided to press charges against Bill.'

'Thanks for saving me the trouble of reading it,' Bridie said drily, taking the card from her receptionist's outstretched hand.

'Sorry.' Fiona smiled without rancour. For a few moments she busied herself in an apparent search for something on the desk and then cleared her throat. 'Jack will be pleased to hear Elsa's happy.'

'I expect so.'

It wasn't exactly the most auspicious response in the world, and Bridie's set features scarcely encouraged further conversation, but Fiona refused to be daunted. 'Have you told Jack that Will Martin can't take the job?'

'No.'

'Don't you think you should?' Fiona exclaimed with a mixture of exasperation and concern. 'You're really going to be stretched on your own, and there's a limit to what Bob Maxwell can do to help—he has his own practice to consider, remember?'

Bridie finished packing her medical bag with supplies and then closed it with a snap. 'I'll manage.'

'Oh, yes?' Fiona retorted. 'I'll remind you of that

in a month's time, when you're half-dead on your feet through exhaustion!'

'If you're quite finished with your opinions as to what I should and shouldn't do, I'd like those letters inviting attendance for a cervical smear to go out today.'

Fiona hesitated for a second and then drew herself up to her full five feet nothing. 'No, I'm not finished,' she declared determinedly. 'Jack's been mooning round the place like some lovesick schoolboy for days, and you've been biting his head off every time he tries to speak to you. He's leaving today, Bridie—*today*! Why don't you tell him you love him, that you want him to stay?'

'And why don't you mind your own business?' Bridie replied evenly.

'But you love him, and I'm damn sure he loves you—what's the problem?'

Bridie's eyebrows rose. 'You mean to tell me you haven't heard the latest juicy piece of gossip yet? My, oh, my, but the grapevine's surely slipping.'

Fiona gazed at her with genuine bewilderment. 'I don't know what you're talking about,' she protested. 'All I do know is that you're letting the best thing that's ever happened to you walk away, and I could hit you!'

'Finished?' Bridie declared, her eyes hard.

Fiona's decidedly unladylike oath as she went out of the door was her answer.

Bridie lifted her coffee-cup with a shaking hand and took a gulp. The coffee was stone-cold but she forced it down. Somehow she had got through these last few days, and she would get through today too.

But today's different; today he's leaving, a little voice whispered. I'll survive, she told herself; I always have done. But at what price? the little voice demanded. What price?

She had only ever loved and completely trusted four men in her life, and three of them had betrayed that trust. Only Andrew had been honest with her; only Andrew had not let her down willingly. A tear trickled down her cheek and she brushed it away angrily. Tears achieved nothing; tears were a weakness.

'No more, Bridie,' she muttered. 'No more.' If she had learned nothing else it was that only the strong survived.

'I've got some great news about John Harvey, Bridie!'

Somehow she managed to smile as Jack strode into the room, clear elation on his face.

'We know what's wrong with him at last—he's got brucellosis.'

'How in the world—?'

'Do you remember telling me that John had only just recently bought the dairy farm?' he said eagerly, sitting down on the edge of her desk. 'It rang a bell in my head because I dealt with a case of brucellosis years ago in France. The symptoms weren't quite the same—they never are with brucellosis—so I asked the boffins in the blood lab to run some additional checks and it's just been confirmed.'

'Yes, but how—?'

'Apparently John got into the habit of occasionally taking a mug of milk from one of the churns before they went off to be pasteurised, not realising just how dangerous it could be. Luckily—or unluckily—none of the rest of the family ever drank any of the unpasteurised milk, so they showed no symptoms. If they'd all drunk it we might have caught on quicker.'

'Congratulations,' she said. 'You must be thrilled to bits to have cracked the case just before you left.'

The smile on his face faded and she glanced away,

cursing her own stupidity. Why had she said that? Why hadn't she kept her mouth shut? She'd given him the opening he needed.

'I don't have to leave, Bridie,' he said quietly.

'John will need a full course of antibiotics, I suppose?' she said swiftly, deliberately changing the subject.

He nodded. 'It will be a pretty long haul, what with us having taken so long to work out what was wrong with him, but in time he should make a full recovery.' He paused, his eyes fixed on hers. 'As I said, I don't have to leave.'

'It's for the best,' she said briskly. 'Now, I know you won't be here when I come back from my rounds so I want to wish you the very best of luck—'

'Will you stop with these platitudes?' he demanded, his voice harsh. 'Why won't you believe me when I say I was never involved in Neil Jardine's stupid betting-ring?'

'Have you got all your clothes packed?'

'Bridie, listen to me—'

'I should have listened to you before,' she said, her face bitter. 'You told me that nothing ever lasts, didn't you—that the only way to survive this life is to depend on no one, trust no one? I should have listened to you then. I didn't, but I've learned the rules now, Jack; I've learned the rules.'

He gazed at her in despair. 'I was wrong, Bridie. I was so very wrong. That isn't living; that's just existing. I love you—'

The force of her hand across his cheek silenced him.

'You don't know the meaning of the word!' she cried, all the hurt and anger she had been trying so desperately to suppress suddenly erupting. 'Can you imagine what it felt like to sit and listen to you tell Andrew the day after we had made love that you didn't want to stay on here? Can you even *begin* to imagine how that felt?

'But then you didn't make love to me, did you, Jack?' she continued, her voice breaking. 'You and I had sex; that was all it was, wasn't it? Even I know the difference—even naïve, inexperienced, stupid Bridie McEwen knows the difference. You make love to someone you love, and you have sex with someone you want.'

'Bridie—'

'But then love's just a meaningless word to you, isn't it?' she said, dashing a shaking hand across her cheek as a tear trickled down it. 'It's not a real emotion, just a polite euphemism for wanting to bed someone. You warned me not to fall in love with you, didn't you? But you're so good, Jack; you're so good,' she added, her lips twisting into a smile.

'All it took was a little bit of kindness and you actually had *me* asking *you* to make love to me. That's the really funny part of all this—the really side-splittingly funny part. You didn't have to do anything. I was the one who begged you to take me to bed!'

'Don't, Bridie—oh, please don't do this,' he said, his voice raw with emotion, his eyes dark with pain. 'I've been a fool, I admit it. It's taken me too long to discover how I feel about you but can't you trust me? Can't you believe me when I say I love you?'

'I could have—once—but the trust has all gone, Jack—all gone,' she replied, her face cold.

'It can come back—if you want it to,' he said hoarsely. 'You can start by believing me and not that little creep Neil Jardine; you can trust me and not him.'

'It's too late.'

'It's never too late,' he insisted. 'I've learned how to trust. I never thought it was possible to say to another human being, This is my heart. Take it—it's yours to do with as you want. But I have, Bridie; I have.'

She wanted to believe him, but she was so hurt, so humiliated still, and slowly she shook her head. 'It's too late, Jack.'

He tried to take her in his arms and she pushed him away angrily. 'You just don't get it, do you?' she said fiercely. 'I can't bear you near me now, Jack; I can't even bear the sight of you!'

'Bridie—'

'Just. . .just go away, and leave me alone!'

She heard him sigh, and then she heard the sound of the door closing quietly behind him as he went out. A small sob broke from her and she bit her lip savagely. She was not going to cry—no matter how she felt, she was not going to cry.

Quickly she picked up her list of morning calls. Work—she could lose herself in her work. It had always eased her emptiness and unhappiness in the past; it could do so again.

It did not take her long to discover, however, that it was a vain hope. Every patient she called on wanted to sympathise over Jack's departure—from young Kate Jennings who was worried about her baby, to old Mrs Munroe who had a bad attack of shingles—and each and every one of them gazed at her thoughtfully, as though they could read the misery on her face.

She got through her rounds mechanically—automatically changing dressings, sounding chests, checking blood pressures—but all the time her brain kept on repeating, I want to go home; I want to hide in my room and never come out again until everyone has forgotten Jack Culrain ever came to the village.

By the time she was heading back to Struan she was physically and emotionally exhausted, but the peace she had hoped for was not to be. Just as she reached the hill above the village she recognised Simon's car coming towards her and slowed down immediately.

'You're well out of your usual territory,' she said, rolling down her window wearily. 'Something wrong?'

'Depends on your perspective,' he replied. 'I want to talk to you.'

She glanced down the road. 'We can't talk here—we'd block the road. There's a lay-by about a mile up the road—'

'I know it.'

'Then turn your car round and follow me there. Oh, and Simon,' she added as he began to accelerate, 'this had better be good—I've had a long day and I'm tired.'

He smiled enigmatically and she drove away quickly, reaching the lay-by a good five minutes ahead of him.

'So what's the problem, then?' she asked as he got out of his car.

'I've been down to the house to say goodbye to Jack. He was putting his suitcase in that old rust-bucket he laughingly describes as a car when I left.'

'So?' she said coolly.

'You're not going to stop him?'

Angry colour flooded across Bridie's cheeks. 'Since when was it any of your business what I did?'

'Since you gave me the privilege of accepting me as a friend,' he replied calmly.

She gazed out at the countryside before her, at the hills and fields, the small village of Struan nestling in the valley below them, and sighed. 'I'm sure you mean well, Simon, but please, just drop the subject, will you?'

'I would if I thought you knew what you were doing, but I don't think you do,' he observed. 'Tell him you want him to stay, Bridie.'

'Why does everyone assume I'm Jack's keeper?' she

exclaimed. 'First it's Fiona and now it's you. Jack's a grown man, a free agent—he can go where he likes.'

'And you know very well he'd like to stay on here. You're cutting off your nose to spite your face, you know that, don't you?'

She sat down on the grass, clasping her knees close to her chest. 'If that's all you came to say you could have saved your petrol.'

He picked up a small stone, examined it thoughtfully for a moment, and then hurled it down the slope. 'I always knew you were as stubborn as a mule,' he declared. 'I didn't know you were bloody stupid as well.'

She glared up at him and then, despite herself, a small chuckle broke from her. 'You don't even like Jack, Simon.'

'I don't,' he said as he sat down on the grass beside her, 'but then I wouldn't like anyone you fell in love with.'

His grey eyes saw too much, she thought, and she glanced away from him quickly, only to hear him sigh.

'I thought you knew Jack better than this, Bridie.'

'I know him as well as I want to, thank you,' she said crisply.

He pulled her round to face him, and to her surprise there was real anger on his face. 'You honestly think he'd make love to you for a bet?'

'So it's common knowledge now, is it?' she said, ice-cold, though her cheeks were hot with mounting colour. 'The talk of the wards, the canteen—'

'No, it isn't common knowledge,' he replied in exasperation. 'I only know about it because Neil Jardine has asked me to arrange a transfer for him to another hospital. Whatever Neil's faults are, he's a good doctor, Bridie, and I refused to agree to arrange the transfer until he told me why he wanted the move.

He's terrified witless of what Jack might do to him.'

'Good,' she replied tersely.

'I can guarantee no one will ever refer to this betting episode again,' he continued. 'There's nothing to tell anyway, since Jack point-blank refuses to say whether he's slept with you or not.'

'Am I supposed to be grateful for that?' she retorted.

He shook his head. 'Bitterness is a very destructive emotion, Bridie. For God's sake don't throw away your chance of happiness because of a misunderstanding, and certainly not because of misplaced pride. True happiness doesn't come round that often, my dear.'

'Is that it—are you finished?' she asked, her face set.

'Bloody-minded, aren't you?' he said, with a half-smile.

'I know what I'm doing, if that's what you mean,' she replied.

'I doubt that,' he said as he got to his feet. 'Tell me something, Bridie.'

'What?'

'Are you happy? Think about it, my dear. Think long and hard, because if you aren't you've still got time to make it right.'

She sat for a long time looking down over Struan after Simon had driven away. The leaves and bracken were already beginning to show their autumn colours. There was a sharpness in the air in the mornings now that foretold that autumn would soon be here.

She shivered slightly and it was not with cold, for the early autumn sun was still warm. What did she have to look forward to when winter came but a lonely bed and a succession of locums, until she found someone who could step into Andrew's shoes? And it would have to be Andrew's shoes—no one would ever take Jack's place.

She got to her feet stiffly. It was too late for regrets.

Jack would already have left for London. She would get over him—she had to; she had no other choice.

She drove home slowly, reluctant to go back to the house, but when she reached Struan's main street Mrs Dunn waved her down and she came to a halt quickly.

'What's happened?' she asked, switching off her ignition. 'Is something wrong with Jamie?'

Mrs Dunn's face was a mixture of conflicting emotions. 'I could kill him, Doctor, I really could. I don't know why he has to get up to such mischief. I only left him for a minute—'

'What's he done?' Bridie interrupted gently.

'You're never going to believe this, Doctor, but he's got his head stuck through the railings outside the chemist!'

Bridie began to laugh. 'You'd better take me to him.'

'We've called out the fire brigade,' Jamie's mother declared as she led the way across the street, 'but I'm worried in case he has an asthma attack, though Dr Culrain says—'

Bridie came to a halt. 'Jack—Dr Culrain's here?'

'I was surprised too!' Mrs Dunn exclaimed. 'I thought he was leaving today—'

'We'd better see how Jamie's getting on,' Bridie broke in. She didn't want to talk about Jack; her emotions were still too raw for that.

Quite a crowd had gathered round Jamie, all offering advice and suggestions. In fact, the only person who seemed totally unconcerned by the situation was Jamie himself, who was busily licking an ice cream that had been donated by one of the concerned onlookers.

'Any suggestions?' Jack asked, with a broad grin as soon as he saw her.

'As he managed to get his head through in the first place he should be able to get it out again,' she said thoughtfully, bending down and smiling at Jamie.

'Unfortunately everyone's had a shot at freeing him, and now his neck is a lot more swollen that it was,' Jack replied ruefully.

'What on earth's all this?' She grimaced, touching the sticky yellow mass around Jamie's neck gingerly.

'A mixture of lard and butter,' Jack replied ruefully. 'That's just one of the many things that's been tried.'

She stood up. 'Any trouble with his breathing?' she asked in an undertone.

'None at all,' he said. 'In fact, apart from the fact he's got his head stuck through the railings, he's right as rain. My advice is to stand by in readiness but do nothing until the fire brigade arrive—they're the experts in this sort of thing.'

She nodded, and crouched down again so that her head was level with Jamie's. 'I'm afraid it looks as though you're going to be here a little bit longer, Jamie. Do you think you can be brave for just a few minutes more?'

''Course I can,' Jamie said stoutly. 'I'm no' afraid of nothing.'

'Well done,' she smiled.

'Can I ask you something, Doctor?' he continued, licking his ice cream pensively. 'My mum told my dad that you'd been dumped by Dr Culrain. What does dumped mean?'

An embarrassed silence fell over the crowd of onlookers and Bridie gazed at the pavement, her cheeks crimson.

'Is it a naughty word?' Jamie asked, colouring almost as much as Bridie . 'If it is—'

'It's not a naughty word,' Jack said calmly, getting down on his knees in front of him. 'Being dumped by someone simply means you don't like them any more. But I'm afraid your mother got it wrong,' he added, pitching his voice deliberately louder. 'Dr McEwen dumped me.'

A ripple of whispered comment ran round the crowd—comment that was only halted by the arrival of the fire brigade.

'There's no need for you to wait, Jack,' Bridie murmured as the fire brigade set to work with much good-humoured banter. 'I know you have a long journey ahead of you.'

He nodded, and her heart contracted as he walked away. She couldn't let him go like this; she couldn't just let him walk out of her life. She called out his name and he turned eagerly, and so did half the crowd. 'Good. . .good luck with the job in America, Jack.'

His eyes met hers. She loved him; she was never going to love anyone as much as she loved him. All she had to do was say it, but she couldn't—the words just wouldn't come. Too much had happened for her to be able to lay her heart bare in public.

She stared at him silently, willing him to make the first move, knowing that if he would only say that he loved her then she would fly into his arms, but he didn't say he loved her, he just waved a salute and got into his car.

'That's the wee fella free now, Doc!' one of the firemen shouted.

She turned towards the fireman uncertainly, and heard the sound of Jack's car spluttering into life.

'I'm afraid he's got a couple of abrasions to his neck,' the fireman continued. 'We tried to be as careful as possible, but the railings were pretty rusty.'

She nodded, and heard the roar of the ancient exhaust.

'Are you coming, Doc?' the fireman asked, staring at her in clear bewilderment.

She had a job to do; people were depending on her.

'Yes,' she said as the sound of the exhaust grew fainter and fainter. 'Yes, I'm coming.'

'Where's Dr Culrain?' Jamie asked, his large brown eyes fixed on her curiously as she dressed the wounds on his neck and then sounded his thin chest.

'He had to go,' she replied with difficulty.

'Is he coming back?' he pressed.

'No.'

'Your face has gone all funny,' he observed thoughtfully, 'and your eyes are red, like when you have a cold—'

'Try and keep him quiet for the rest of the day if you can, Mrs Dunn,' she said, turning to Jamie's mother quickly. 'He should be fine but I think he's had more than enough excitement for one day.' Mrs Dunn nodded. 'And as for you, young man,' Bridie added, smiling tremulously at Jamie. 'No more experiments with railings—promise?'

'Promise.' He grinned.

'Is that Dr Culrain away now, Dr McEwen?' Mrs Jones from the corner grocery asked regretfully as Bridie pushed her way through the onlookers, who were already beginning to disperse, the excitement of the morning over.

'It is,' Bridie replied, trying to sidestep her without success.

'He was a nice young fellow,' Mrs Jones observed. 'His clothes were a bit—well—unorthodox, but, as I said to my Fred, you don't judge a book by its cover, do you?'

Bridie shook her head.

'So who'll be taking Dr Weston's place, then?'

'No one at the moment. I have interviews to conduct next week.'

Mrs Jones sighed. 'Long queues in the waiting room, then, for the foreseeable future?'

'Afraid so. Now, if you'll excuse me. . .?'

'Of course, of course,' Mrs Jones agreed. 'It's a shame, though, isn't it—about Dr Culrain?'

Bridie muttered something unintelligible in reply and fled.

At least she had no evening surgery ahead of her, she thought with relief when she reached home and closed the front door wearily behind her. Bob Maxwell had agreed to provide emergency cover for the night, so the whole evening was hers. To do what with? a little voice whispered—a little voice she deliberately subdued.

She was so tired—so very tired. She would have liked to sleep for a week, to forget everything, but all she had was this one night to pull herself together in preparation for what she knew would be a stream of inquisitions from her patients tomorrow.

Fiona, she thought quickly; Fiona would cheer her up. But her office was empty and there was a note taped to the door: 'Had to go out—have fun!' Have *fun*? What fun could she have in a house that suddenly seemed too big—a house that felt intimidating and cold instead of friendly and welcoming as it used to be.

Slowly she made her way towards the stairs and then stopped. If she hadn't known better she would have sworn that she could smell food cooking. She breathed in deeply. There *was* food cooking—bacon and eggs. Someone was cooking bacon and eggs, and she knew only one person whose speciality that was.

She raced up the stairs, her heart soaring, and pushed open the kitchen door. A frying-pan sat on the stove, sizzling with bacon and eggs, but the kitchen was empty. Quickly she took the pan off the stove, a slight frown creasing her forehead, and then wheeled round as she heard a movement behind her. From round the kitchen door came an old broom-handle with a white handkerchief tied to it.

'Jack?' she exclaimed uncertainly, taking a half-step forward and then stopping.

He put his head round the door, looking thoroughly nervous.

'What's this?' she asked, indicating the stick and handkerchief in his hands.

'A flag of truce, surrender—call it what you will,' he answered.

'I. . .I thought you'd gone,' she said as he put the makeshift flag down on the table.

'I couldn't. I know you told me to go, that you didn't want or need me, but the trouble is I've discovered I need you. . .very badly.'

'Jack—'

'Let me finish,' he interrupted, his voice cracking. 'I love you, Bridie McEwen; I always will love you. I'm not taking that job in the States. I'm going to rent a house in the village and try and get work at Perth. I'm going to dog your every footstep, hang around you like some lovesick spaniel until you see I really do love you. I'll wait for you, little one, if it takes a lifetime.'

A half-laugh, half-sob broke from her, and when he opened his arms to her she crossed the kitchen quickly and rushed into them. 'Oh, Jack, I'm sorry; I'm so sorry,' she whispered. 'I've been such an idiot—such a stupid idiot.'

He looked down at her, his face so tender but his eyes still uncertain. 'Does that mean you want me to stay?'

She stretched up and smoothed his hair back from his forehead, her eyes large and luminous. 'That means I love you, Jack,' she smiled.

His lips sought hers hungrily and she responded with equal need, locking her arms around his neck to bring him closer. It seemed so long—so long since she had felt the sweetness of his mouth on hers, so long since she had revelled in the gentle strength of his arms around her. But as their kisses deepened and his hands began to arouse her she extricated herself gently from his arms and sighed regretfully.

'We can't, Jack—not yet. Fiona will be back—'

'Not tonight, she won't.' He grinned. 'I persuaded her to go home.'

Her eyebrows rose. 'Did you indeed? Now, how on earth did you manage that?'

'With a pair of strong hands and a few—how shall I phrase this?—expressive observations!' He chuckled.

She laughed. 'So that's why her note urged me to "have fun".'

'If she said that I think we should try our best to oblige, don't you?' he asked, clasping her hand in his and leading her out of the kitchen and across the hall.

She went with him willingly, but when they reached his room she paused momentarily. Sensing her nervousness, he put his hand under her chin, tilting it gently towards him. 'I won't hurt you—you know that, don't you?' he said softly. 'I promised you—oh, what seems like a lifetime ago now—that the next time would be perfect, and it will be; it will be.'

She nodded and began to undo the buttons on her blouse, but her fingers were awkward, clumsy.

'Let me do that—please,' he murmured.

She swallowed and stood motionless, though every part of her trembled as he removed her clothes slowly, without haste, until she was naked before him.

'You're so beautiful, Bridie,' he said huskily, sliding his hands up to cup her breasts and lowering his head to tease the nipples into an aching hardness with his tongue.

His hands travelled downwards, and she moaned

softly as a myriad shuddering sensations flooded through her. Quickly she reached out to slip off his shirt, his trousers, until he was as naked as she.

Gently he lowered her onto the bed, and she felt no fear, no panic. All she felt was an overwhelming longing for him—for all of him—a longing that grew ever more intense with every caress of his fingers, every intimate touch of his lips and mouth.

She knew without being experienced that he was arousing her with infinite patience, that he was holding himself in check, waiting for her. But very soon she did not want him to wait—very soon her body was crying out for release, and she heard her own voice calling as though from a great distance 'Now, Jack, now!'

And as he joined with her it came—such a surge of spiralling sensations, such an explosion of pulsing force that she cried out again, this time in ecstasy, knowing that at last she was whole, that Jack had made her complete, that the joining had not just been one of bodies but of minds and souls.

'Wow!' Jack declared as he gathered her into his arms later and smoothed her damp hair back from her forehead. 'When you said you were a quick learner you weren't kidding!'

Bridie chuckled and leant back against his chest, knowing that at last she had come home.

'There's just one thing,' he observed, nuzzling her ear thoughtfully. 'I'm afraid we got a bit carried away and I forgot to take any precautions, so I think we'd better get married as quickly as possible.'

'Married?' she echoed, turning round to face him, her face showing her surprise.

'It seems a good idea, don't you think?'

She thought it was the most wonderful idea in the

world, but this was the first, and she knew it would also be the only proposal she would ever receive, so she appeared to consider it carefully. 'It's a big step, Jack,' she observed, resting her chin on his chest, 'though it would solve the partnership question.'

'Hey, whoever said women were the romantic sex?' he protested. 'To hell with the partnership; I'm talking about you and me here. Don't you want to marry me?' His face was uncertain, anxious.

'Of course I want to marry you,' she said softly, and then ducked her head as her lips curved into a smile. 'Will Martin's going to be very disappointed, though. I don't suppose we could engage him as a locum, could we? He has such excellent qualifications, and, as Fiona said, he's also rather cute.'

His grip on her tightened. 'I have absolutely no intention of employing a man that my future wife thinks is cute!'

'Don't tell me you don't trust me, Jack?' she said, gazing up at him in wide-eyed innocence.

He captured her chin quickly, and as he saw the laughter lurking at the back of her eyes his lips twitched. 'I can see that the sooner you're safely married to me, the better!'

'You won't hire Will Martin, then?' she sighed, playing with the hair on his chest.

'There will be no more locums, full stop,' he said firmly.

'Pity,' she observed.

'Why?'

'Well, locums can turn out to be such interesting, attractive men,' she said slyly, and then shrieked with laughter as he rolled her onto her back and proceeded to demonstrate again just how very interesting locums could be.

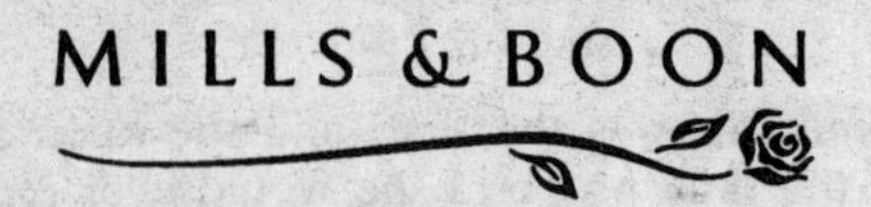

MEDICAL ROMANCE

LOVE ON CALL

The books for enjoyment this month are:

AND DAUGHTER MAKES THREE	Caroline Anderson
A QUESTION OF TRUST	Maggie Kingsley
THE DISTURBING DR SHELDON	Elisabeth Scott
CONSULTANT CARE	Sharon Wirdnam

Treats in store!

Watch next month for the following absorbing stories:

BUSH DOCTOR'S BRIDE	Marion Lennox
FORGOTTEN PAIN	Josie Metcalfe
COUNTRY DOCTORS	Gill Sanderson
COURTING DR GROVES	Meredith Webber

Available from W.H. Smith, John Menzies, Volume One, Forbuoys, Martins, Woolworths, Tesco, Asda, Safeway and other paperback stockists.

Readers in South Africa - write to:
IBS, Private Bag X3010, Randburg 2125.

GET 4 BOOKS AND A MYSTERY GIFT

Return this coupon and we'll send you 4 Love on Call novels and a mystery gift absolutely FREE! We'll even pay the postage and packing for you.

We're making you this offer to introduce you to the benefits of Reader Service: FREE home delivery of brand-new Love on Call novels, at least a month before they are available in the shops, FREE gifts and a monthly Newsletter packed with information.

Accepting these FREE books and gift places you under no obligation to buy, you may cancel at any time, even after receiving just your free shipment. Simply complete the coupon below and send it to:

MILLS & BOON READER SERVICE, FREEPOST, CROYDON, SURREY, CR9 3WZ.

No stamp needed

Yes, please send me 4 free Love on Call novels and a mystery gift. I understand that unless you hear from me, I will receive 4 superb new titles every month for just £2.10* each postage and packing free. I am under no obligation to purchase any books and I may cancel or suspend my subscription at any time, but the free books and gifts will be mine to keep in any case. (I am over 18 years of age)

1EP6D

Ms/Mrs/Miss/Mr ______________________________

Address ______________________________

____

______________ Postcode ______________

Offer closes 30th September 1996. We reserve the right to refuse an application. *Prices and terms subject to change without notice. Offer only valid in UK and Ireland and is not available to current subscribers to this series. **Readers in Ireland please write to: P.O. Box 4546, Dublin 24.** Overseas readers please write for details.

You may be mailed with offers from other reputable companies as a result of this application. Please tick box if you would prefer not to receive such offers. ☐

MILLS & BOON

Bestselling romances brought back to you by popular demand

Don't miss our sizzling April title

Father Knows Last

Two handsome, unmarried men are about to get the surprise of their lives... Well better late than never!

Two complete novels in one romantic volume by Emma Darcy and Jacqueline Baird.

Available: April 1996 Price: £4.50

Available from WH Smith, John Menzies, Volume One, Forbuoys, Martins, Woolworths, Tesco, Asda, Safeway and other paperback stockists.